DRAGON
ON THE MOUNTAIN

Madeline Rose

ANGUS
& ROBERTSON
PUBLISHERS

BY THE SAME AUTHOR
Witch Over the Water
Witch In the Bush
The Secret of Shelter Bay

ANGUS & ROBERTSON PUBLISHERS

Unit 4, Eden Park, 31 Waterloo Road,
North Ryde, NSW, Australia 2113, and
16 Golden Square, London WIR 4BN,
United Kingdom

First published in Australia
by Angus & Robertson Publishers in 1987
First published in the United Kingdom
by Angus & Robertson (UK) in 1987

National Library of Australia
Cataloguing-in-publication data.

Rose, Madeline, 1932- .
  Dragon on the mountain.

  ISBN 0 207 15107 5.

  I. Davy, Mary. II. Title.

A823'.3

Typeset in 14 pt Plantin by Midland Typesetters
Printed in Australia by The Book Printer

CONTENTS

1 OFF TO THE MOUNTAINS

The station wagon bowled swiftly along the dirt road, churning up a cloud of red dust. A laden trailer bumped along behind it. On every side stretched brownish fields, scattered with grey-green trees.

The four children, sharing the back of the car with a large dog, watched the landscape eagerly and wriggled from time to time with excitement. But they kept quiet. Their mother was in a very bad mood.

"What made you do it, William?" asked Mrs Ailsa Blair, for the third time that morning. "We were saving that money for a place at the beach. How could you waste it on a shack in the mountains?"

"I keep explaining," replied Mr Blair. "You just don't listen. It would have taken years to save enough for a beach house. This place was very

1

cheap and fully furnished too. Besides, I like the mountains."

"It was cheap because no one wanted it," stormed Mrs Blair. "A hovel miles and miles from anywhere. If it had to be a weekender in the mountains, why not somewhere where the children could have learned to ski? There'll be no chance of that where we're going. It's far too rough. And there won't be anyone to talk to either!"

"I wanted somewhere quiet to write my book," said Mr Blair stubbornly. "Cheer up, Ailsa! I'm sure you'll like it when you see it."

"You haven't even seen it yourself!" retorted Mrs Blair. "How could you buy it when you've only seen a photo?"

Behind his mother's back, Paul, the eldest, quietly slid the same photograph from the pocket in the car door. The children passed it from hand to hand, frowning at the blurred print and protecting it from the questioning nose of Lula the dog, as they tried to make out the details. It was a distant view of a squarish building, huddled against the side of a mountain. The slopes above looked wild and barren.

The road widened briefly and Mr Blair stopped the car with a jerk outside a small store with a lone petrol pump. A few shabby buildings were scattered on either side of the road. Mrs Blair glanced at the map.

"We'll be branching right soon, up into the mountains. This is the last little town we'll see. Perhaps the children would like a milkshake."

"A cuppa for me," said Mr Blair, stretching his arms and yawning.

Lula sprang from the back of the wagon.

"Don't bring her into the shop," said Mrs Blair. "Pop her back in the car. We'll leave the windows half-open."

Paul grabbed Lula's collar and Tania rushed to help him. Between them they pushed and coaxed the reluctant dog back into the car. Ellen and Jim, the two younger children, were already inside the store, choosing the flavours for their milkshakes.

It was rather stuffy in the little shop, but the milk was fresh and cold. The children drank thirstily, then chased stray bubbles round the cool metal tumblers. Their mother was at the grocery shelves, peering at tickets and labels. Their father was drinking his tea and reading yesterday's newspaper. The old woman behind the counter looked curiously at the children, as she mopped up some spilt milk.

"We don't get many people through here, these days. Where are you making for?"

"We're going up into the hills over there," said Tania. "Up to the right, a little way along the road."

"But there's nothing up there!" said the shopkeeper, stopping with her cloth in mid-wipe. "It's just a fire trail, then a rough track. Leads nowhere. It's a dead end."

"There's a house there," said Paul. "We have a picture of it." He pulled the photograph from his pocket and held it across the counter. The old woman adjusted the spectacles on her nose and looked closely at the picture.

"Ah," she said suddenly. "I know what that'll be! That's McPherson's old shack. Properly out in the wilds that is. Nobody's lived there for a long time. McPherson died, must be five years ago, up in Queensland. The son came down a while ago to clean up the house and patch the roof. Said he was going to put it on the market. Thought some simple soul might buy it as a weekender."

Tania glanced uneasily at her father, but he seemed absorbed in his newspaper.

"We bought it! We bought it!" said Ellen, dancing up and down. "Well, Dad did, while we were away visiting Grandma."

"You'll not get much use out of it," said the old woman doubtfully. "It's very cold up there, even in summer. And in winter that track often gets blocked by snow."

Ellen and Jim had never seen snow. They listened eagerly. "When does it start snowing?" asked Ellen.

"Not for another three months at least. You should be safe enough up there for now. But once the falls start, you'll have to forget the place till the spring."

Jim was disappointed. "Won't we see any snow at all?"

"We're here for three weeks," said Ellen hopefully.

"Not a chance," said the old woman. "That is . . . unless you find the place where the snow never melts."

"Never melts?" asked Paul.

"Oh, it's just a story," said the shopkeeper. "When I was a child we were always searching, but we never found it. In those days there was an old Aborigine living in that hut at the end of the street. He told us about this place, hidden in the mountains, so high and cold that the snow didn't melt there, even in the middle of summer. We used to sneak off, without telling our parents, to look for it. I was lost up there once or twice. Earned some nasty hidings. But we never found it. We kept asking old Bill to give us directions, but he just sat back and roared with laughter. Said it was just as well not to find the place; that it was guarded by monsters."

"Monsters?" asked Jim, who tended to dream about dinosaurs. His mother, placing some milk cartons on the counter, noticed his face. She had heard the shopkeeper's last few words.

"There are no monsters in Australia!" she said briskly.

"Just a story, like I said," muttered the old woman, adding up the cost of the milk.

Outside the store, Mrs Blair loosened the cover of the trailer and jammed the cartons into a corner. The trailer was packed with food, clothes, sleeping-bags, blankets, a big box of candles, and all sorts of other things the Blairs thought they might need. The shopkeeper had followed them outside. She craned her neck trying to see the contents of the trailer.

"You won't want to be up there long," she said. "It seems to turn people funny. Mr McPherson went right off his head. And then of course there's Mad Wally."

"Mad Wally?" exclaimed Mrs Blair in alarm. "What sort of place is this, William?"

Her husband glared at the shopkeeper. "Come on, kids," he said. "It's time we were on our way. Into the car. Hurry up now!"

He opened the car door and gave a shout of rage. Lula looked at him guiltily; the half-chewed map dropped from her mouth. "Why didn't you stick that back in the glove box, Ailsa?"

"It's all right," said Tania, smoothing out the damp, tattered paper. "The bit we need is still here."

The Blairs climbed back into their seats and Mr Blair started the motor. "You're not doing much of a job, training that animal," he growled. "When I said you could have a dog, you promised to see it was well behaved. As it is, nothing's safe. Nothing! Well heaven help her if she ever gets hold of my manuscripts."

"I think she must be teething," said Paul. "She's only a puppy still, Dad."

"Teething? Nonsense!" shouted Mr Blair, slamming the gear lever. "She has teeth like a crocodile."

The shopkeeper crossed to the car and put her face to the open window. "Have you any other pets with you?"

"No," snapped Mr Blair.

The woman stood back and folded her arms. "Well, you'll be all right with Mad Wally then, won't you?"

The car roared away. "What did she mean? Who is this Mad Wally?" asked Mrs Blair nervously. "I don't like the sound of him at all."

"That woman is just an old gossip!" said Mr Blair. "I've heard of this Wally person—the agent mentioned him. He's an old man who used to work for the Parks and Wildlife. Lives halfway up the road."

"But is he mad?" asked Paul.

His father shrugged his shoulders. "Who's to

say who's mad and who isn't? Mr Swindles assured me that Wally's perfectly harmless."

Jim listened with his mouth open. Ellen squeezed Tania's hand and whispered, "Why did she say that about pets?"

2 MAD WALLY

The track was narrow, winding and very steep. The children glanced back anxiously at the laden trailer, as the car swung round some of the sharper bends. Often potholes or small boulders made it lurch wildly and twice they had to stop to remove fallen branches from the road.

They wound higher and higher. The road was lined thickly with forest and in the tangled undergrowth the children glimpsed unfamiliar plants and flowers.

As they drove on, they began to shiver. Mr Blair closed his window and switched on the car heater. Mrs Blair handed out warm pullovers. "You'd never think it was summer!" she muttered crossly.

Rounding a bend, they were suddenly confronted by someone standing right in the middle of the track; a short square someone, waving a shotgun. Jim dived down behind the front seats. The stranger had a jutting, white beard and a brown, woolly hat.

"It must be Mad Wally," said Mrs Blair faintly.

Mr Blair stopped the car with a jerk. To his annoyance he saw a chain, looped over two tree stumps, blocking their way. "He can't do this!" he spluttered.

Mad Wally thrust his face close to the windscreen and looked rapidly round the station wagon. The children could see his eyeballs, crisscrossed with tiny red lines. He waved at Mr Blair to wind down his window.

"Where are they?" he bellowed. "Where are you hiding them?"

Mr Blair, who had been ready to complain about the chain, was completely taken aback. "What are you talking about?"

"Your cats, of course!" roared Wally.

"Cats?" said Mr Blair, bewildered. "*Cats*?"

"Don't tell me you don't have any," scoffed Wally. "You can't hoodwink me! Families like yours always have cats."

Everyone stared at him, dumbfounded.

"We do have one cat," said Tania.

"She's at home," said Paul.

"She's called Mittens," said Ellen. "Mrs Queeks is looking after her."

"A likely story!" said Mad Wally. "You can't fool me. You're the sort of people who take their cats on holiday. I can tell just by looking at you."

He waved his gun in the air. They thought for a moment he was about to smash the windscreen.

"Well, you're wrong," said Mr Blair. "We don't take the cat away with us. It's awkward enough having to bring the dog. Now undo that chain and let us past!"

Mad Wally leaned down and glowered around the car. "They do so much damage you know," he said. "They kill all the wildlife, vicious little beasts!"

Mrs Blair had recovered somewhat and tried to be diplomatic. "Yes . . . yes," she said sweetly. "Feral cats are a real problem. We wouldn't dream of letting any cat of ours run wild in the bush."

"How do I know you're telling the truth?" asked Mad Wally suspiciously, his eyes still roving around the car. "Ha! I saw something move down there. It'll be a cat all right. You're hiding a cat down there behind that seat!"

Jim straightened up, very red-faced. "I'm not a cat," he said.

"People who hide children," said Wally, "are very likely to hide cats. I shall have to give this car a thorough inspection, in the national interest." He brandished the shotgun wildly.

Mr Blair looked warily at the gun. There seemed little chance that Wally was going to let them pass without a struggle so he decided to humour him. "All right," he said to the children. "Hop out quickly and let this gentleman inspect the car. I'll keep an eye on him. You unlatch that chain."

When he saw he was getting his own way, Mad Wally became suddenly friendly. "Let me introduce myself, Madam," he said to Mrs Blair, who was shivering in the cold mountain breeze. "Wallace Crumthorpe, at your service. I won't detain you long. Perhaps you would care to wait in my humble home?" He waved towards a steep bank at the side of the track.

"Your home?" asked Mrs Blair, puzzled. The children stared. Halfway up the bank was a great, level slab of stone, and under it yawned a black hole.

"It's a burrow!" said Ellen. "He lives in a burrow!"

"It's not a burrow, it's a house," said Wally, offended. "The only sort of house worth having— under a stone, safe from the wind and weather."

"I've never heard of anyone living under a stone before," said Tania in surprise.

"It's the only sensible way to live," said Mad Wally. "The wisdom of the natural world. Pick up any stone and you'll find something living under it. Now if you'd care to wait inside —"

"No thank you," said Mrs Blair, hastily. "Come back, children!"

The children were scrambling up the steep bank to inspect the strange house. They could see nothing inside, but a strong, musty smell rose out of the darkness. "Ugh!" said Paul.

The old man heard and glared at them. He turned to Mrs Blair. "It's not only cats that upset the environment. Dogs are bad and children are worse. I hope you'll keep yours well under control."

13

The inspection took a long time. Wally pried into every corner and poked his gun into every nook and cranny. He stood on his head to look under the seats and insisted on opening every box and bag. Once he gave a shout of triumph and scooped a bundle of fur from a suitcase – but it was only Mrs Blair's old winter hat.

"If this had been a cat," he said to Mrs Blair, "you would have been in serious trouble."

"If that had been a cat," said Mrs Blair crossly, "I wouldn't have packed it in a suitcase and stuffed it full of pantihose."

The children watched, trying not to giggle. "Shall I crawl under the car," whispered Ellen, "and give a meow?" Tania managed to grab her just in time.

At last Wallace Crumthorpe was satisfied. He took a piece of chalk from his pocket and marked a small cross on the bonnet of the station wagon. Then he stood aside and waved the car on. Mr Blair looked angrily at the chalk mark, but decided not to start a fresh argument. They drove on up the mountain.

3 THE HOLIDAY HOUSE

In the late afternoon the trees thinned out. The road stopped climbing and dipped into a slight hollow. Suddenly the children saw the house ahead of them, small and square, built of logs, with a steeply pitched tin roof. It stood on a grassy plateau, close against the flank of a mountain. Around them rose other peaks and ridges. The lower hills were green, with outcrops of grey stone. Up above, the slopes looked harsh and rocky.

The car stopped in front of the house and the Blairs climbed out, stiff from the long journey. It was cool, but in this little valley they were sheltered from the wind.

"I believe it's limestone country," said Mr Blair. "There might be caves."

"Let's go and look for one," said Ellen eagerly.

"Plenty of time for that later," said her mother. She stood listening. "I can hear rushing water. Where's it coming from?"

A little way past the house a small waterfall tumbled down from the cliff into a foaming pool. Lula began lapping noisily at the water's edge. A stream ran out of the pool and across the grass. Tania bent down and swished her hand in the water. It was icy.

Mr Blair pointed to some narrow, rusty pipes that ran down the rock at the side of the fall. "There's our piped water . . . fresh and cold, nothing like that flat stuff in the taps at home."

"No," snapped Mrs Blair. "The stuff at home is safe to drink. This will need boiling." She swooped on Jim, who was standing at the edge of the pool, watching the water ripple over the toes of his shoes. "Keep your feet dry for goodness sake!"

The house was roughly furnished and reasonably clean. It had four main rooms and a central passage.

The children wandered from room to room. Lula sniffed in every corner, wagging her tail. Mr Blair prowled around happily. "Two beds short," he said. "It's a good thing we brought those lilos. But there's everything else we need."

"Everything else we need?" cried Mrs Blair. "There's nothing, William, nothing! No shower, no cooker, no fridge, no lamps!"

"Well, we'll fix all that of course," said her husband. "We'll put it right, bit by bit. But just for now we'll have to make do." He dragged a little table across the corridor and placed it next to the window of one of the bedrooms. "There! That's where I'm going to write my novel. Just look at the view! This can be our room, Ailsa."

"I want a cup of tea," said Mrs Blair. "I'm going to the trailer to find the things. Someone had better light a fire. I can't see any other way of boiling a kettle."

The fireplace was large, built of rough-hewn stone, discoloured by smoke. It had hooks and trivets to hang cooking pots, and someone had left a small pile of firewood beside the hearth. Paul and Tania built the fire carefully, with small, dry twigs underneath and thicker wood on top. The fire flared up, crackling and spitting. The children crouched on the threadbare rug and watched the flames; Lula squeezed between Tania and Ellen.

Mrs Blair had found the kettle. She filled it at the little sink in the corner of the kitchen, and balanced it over the fire. Soon the kettle began to hiss and sing.

"I knew it would be rough up here," said Mrs Blair, "but I never dreamed we'd have to cook over an open fire. Keep back, Jim, you'll burn yourself!"

They sat and sipped their tea in the warmth. The kitchen was also the living room. There were two old easy chairs and a shabby couch. By one wall stood a battered table with wooden benches.

Outside it grew colder, as the long shadows of the mountains covered the valley. "We must unload the trailer before it gets dark," said Mr Blair.

The children ran in and out of the house with bags and suitcases, boxes and bundles. They piled them in the kitchen, in the passage and in the bedrooms, while Mrs Blair tried in vain to sort them out.

Jim soon grew tired of fetching and carrying. He opened the window of the bedroom he was to share with Paul and leaned out, looking at the sunset. A great sea of gold floated over the mountains.

"Come on, lazy!" said Tania, tugging his arm. "We've lost the sausages. Come and help find them."

Ellen had packed the sausages inside the big coffeepot. By the time they had been found, pricked and set to sizzle in a pan over the fire, the sunset had faded. Jim went back to his window. He thought he had never seen such blackness — only the stars shone overhead, thousands of pinpricks of cold light.

"This is the life!" murmured Mr Blair, toasting his toes, after supper.

"Oh, William, it's awful!" said his wife. "It's a wilderness. No comforts and no one but us for hundreds of kilometres."

"You're forgetting Mad Wally," said Paul.

"I'd sooner forget him," said Mrs Blair grimly.

4 THE STRANGE FOOTPRINT

Next morning the sky was cloudless and the sun felt quite warm. The grassland stretched before the house in a rough, green circle. The road they had travelled the day before wound over a rise and then down the other side to disappear into the trees. Around the fields rose the lower slopes of the mountains.

"Let's follow the creek and see where it goes," said Tania. She ran off along the bank, followed closely by the others. Lula frolicked ahead, pausing to bark excitedly now and then. The creek rippled and bubbled over smooth pebbles to the far side of the plateau, where it dipped down suddenly in another small waterfall.

They were standing on the edge of a little cliff. Between the grassy field and the mountain ran a deep cleft, crowded with trees and ferns. Down in the dip the creek disappeared in a tunnel of greenery. Lula plunged down the steep slope.

"Come on!" called Paul. Half scrambling, half sliding, the others followed him down. There was thick moss under their feet and the branches above them were twined with creepers. The creek swirled ahead through the green shade.

"It's like a bit of rainforest, tucked away in a hollow," said Tania, touching a hairy, mossy trunk. "This isn't anything like the rest of the bush."

"It's very sheltered and damp down here," said Paul. "Lots of water must trickle down from the mountain."

Ellen was scrambling along the bank, wriggling between trees, climbing over boulders. "It won't be easy to follow the creek," she called. "There's no path at all."

"Of course there's no path!" shouted Jim. "No one ever comes down here."

The children made very slow progress, trampling ferns, tearing down creepers, snapping off small branches. They heaved stepping-stones into some of the muddier spots. Lula forged happily along beside them, splashing in and out of the water, sniffing at mysterious crevices and crannies, and disappearing into the undergrowth for minutes at a time.

"This isn't much good," said Paul, after a while, pulling his shoe from a sticky patch of mud and balancing on a firmer carpet of moss-covered roots. "We'll never get far along here. It's too overgrown."

"Let's give it a bit longer," said Ellen. "There might be something interesting just up ahead." Everything about the little ravine excited her – the gloom, the rushing water, the lush, green growth and the dark rock faces glistening behind the tangle of leaves and creepers.

The trees overhead parted suddenly to let in the sunlight. The creek widened into a pool of calm, glimmering water, lapping at the base of a sheer cliff. Round the edge of the pool were smooth, flat boulders.

"Where does the creek go?" asked Paul, puzzled. There was no stream rippling away from the other side of the pool. The creek seemed to end in this quiet place.

"It must flow away under the mountain," said Tania at last. "It goes underground."

They settled down in the little clearing. Paul skimmed flat stones over the water, trying to make them bounce on the surface. Ellen made tiny boats from nut husks, leaves and twigs and launched them on the pool. Tania built small castles from pebbles.

Jim fiddled with this and that, wading in water above his ankles. Finally he found a strong twig with a sharp broken point and began to peel off the thick mossy cover from the flat rocks at the shadier end of the pool.

"He's making a mess," said Tania, peering up from her tottering castle.

"Oh, leave him alone," said Paul. "It'll soon grow back and it's keeping him quiet."

Later they began to feel hungry and decided that it must be time for lunch. Tania jumped to her feet. "Come on, Jim," she called. "We'd better start back."

Jim was standing gazing at a flat stone, the stick suspended in his hand. "I've found something!" he yelled. "Come and look! It's a footprint."

"We'll be late," said Tania, picking her way across the rocks. Jim was eagerly pulling the matted, green growth from the stone. It peeled away in large wads, revealing a very strange footprint indeed—the marks of three enormous claws with a spur at the heel.

Tania's exclamation brought the others hurrying over. The four children stared at the rock for a moment in silence.

"It's a fossilized footprint," said Paul.

"It must have been made by a giant bird," said Ellen. "I wouldn't like to meet anything that size!"

"A bird that lived hundreds of years ago," said Tania.

"It came down to the stream for a drink," said Paul. "I wonder if there's one like this in the museum. We must have a look, next time we're in town."

At the mention of the museum, Jim looked alarmed.

He started to pick up the scattered, mossy lumps and press them back over the footprint. "It's mine," he said. "I found it and it belongs here. I don't want people taking it away."

"All right," said Paul. "Calm down. We don't need to tell anyone about it."

The journey back along the creek was easier as they now had a rough track to follow. Before long they had climbed out of the little ravine and were walking back across the grass. The sky clouded over and the mountains suddenly looked threatening. Ellen shivered.

"I suppose," she said, glancing behind her uneasily, "something like the bird that made the footprint couldn't still be alive today, lurking around in the mountains?"

"Still alive?" asked Jim, looking very frightened.

Tania burst out laughing. "Don't be ridiculous. Of course it couldn't! That bird must have been enormous. If it still existed, someone would have seen it."

"Not many people come up here," said Ellen. "And the bird might be good at hiding."

"Piffle!" said Paul. "That's a very old footprint. Creatures like that died out millions of years ago."

"What did you do with yourselves this morning?" asked Mr Blair, coming into the kitchen for his lunch.

"We followed the creek downstream," said Paul. "It disappears under the mountain."

"No one ever goes down there," said Ellen. "We had to make a path."

Mr Blair looked thoughtful. "We ought to make a few rules," he said. "It'd be the easiest thing in the world to lose yourselves around here. I think you should stay within sight of the house. That gives you plenty of scope for walking and climbing, and you'll always be able to take your bearings and find your way home."

"I don't want the younger ones wandering away by themselves," said Mrs Blair, carrying a pan of soup to the table, her face flushed from the fire, her hands streaked with soot. "Paul and Tania, you're responsible for Ellen and Jim!"

"Don't tackle any climb that looks difficult," said Mr Blair. "You don't have proper equipment—no special shoes or ropes. Just stick to the easy slopes."

The children drank their soup in silence. They had planned to explore far into the mountains. It sounded very dull to have to keep within sight of the house.

That afternoon the Blairs took the trailer down to the tree line to collect firewood. Paul and Tania helped to heave dead branches into the trailer while Ellen and Jim hunted for twigs and sticks for starting fires. Mr Blair towed several trailer-loads up to the house.

"That should last us more than three weeks," he said. "I'll just chop enough to keep us warm tonight."

"I can't start the dinner until you do," said his wife. "The fire is almost out."

Mr Blair had never used an axe before. He swung it clumsily and his hands soon began to blister. He was amazed at the heaviness of the axe and the hardness of the wood. But he was strong and the blade was new and sharp, so before long he had enough firewood to last the evening.

"Can I have a go at chopping wood tomorrow?" asked Paul, as he poked fresh twigs into the dying ashes.

"Can I?" cried Tania, Ellen and Jim together.

"You wouldn't be able to handle the axe," said Mr Blair. "I made a mistake there. We could have done with something lighter, and a saw would have been useful. I'm afraid chopping wood will have to be my job."

5 LULA FINDS A CAVE

"Let's climb up the mountain above the ravine," said Paul. "Then Dad can't watch us through his bedroom window. It faces the other way." He was still annoyed by the limits that his father had set the day before.

The children struggled up the slope, their feet sometimes slipping on the grass, then they clambered over a rocky outcrop onto a wide ledge. At the back of the ledge was a cliff of sheer, grey rock. At the foot of the cliff grew some dense, prickly bushes.

"Can we stop for a bit?" panted Ellen, flopping down. Paul and Tania stood waiting impatiently. Jim was glad of the rest. He sat on the rim of the ledge, dangling his aching legs.

It was a beautiful morning, the mountain peaks clear against the sky, the distances tinged with blue and purple. Far below them the house looked like a toy, a model built with matchsticks.

"Look," said Jim, "there's Lula! I wonder

27

where she's been." He pointed to a tiny figure, bounding across the mountain towards them. They had not seen the dog since breakfast. She had wandered off around the valley, sniffing and exploring. Since there was no traffic to threaten her and no sheep to excite her, Mrs Blair had said she might as well have her freedom. She was tired of rescuing things from Lula's jaws.

"She's coming to see us," said Ellen.

"No," said Paul. "She's chasing something!" And so she was – something small and brown and furry, with short legs and a long, rat-like tail. As the children watched, it popped up onto the ledge, then froze, staring at them with wild, bright eyes.

"It's all right," said Tania. "We won't hurt you."

The creature did not seem reassured. It glanced frantically around, then streaked between the children, leaping right over Ellen's outstretched legs. She fell backwards with a little shriek, then recovered her balance.

"Where did it go?"

"Under the bushes," said Tania. "It'll be safe in there."

Lula arrived, panting, a moment later. She barked briefly to the children, then resumed the hunt, nosing eagerly across the ledge. She thrust her head under a bush.

"Don't let her catch it," said Jim fearfully.

"She'll never get in there," said Ellen. "It's too thick and thorny."

But the dog was determined. She fought and struggled to push her way under the prickly branches. Paul stepped forward to grab her, but he was too late. Her tail and hindquarters slid out of sight.

"She'll catch it, she'll eat it!" cried Jim. He grabbed a stick and hit out at the bushes. "Come out of there, you bad dog!"

"It's probably hiding in a hole or a crevice," said Tania. "Or it may have run away behind the bushes."

Jim stopped thrashing about with his stick. They listened. There was not a sound: no frantic squealing, no barking, no growling—not even the crackle of twigs and leaves or the rattle of stones.

"*Lula!*" called Tania anxiously. There was no answering bark, just complete silence. They looked to left and right, then up at the grey face of the cliff. "She's vanished!" said Ellen.

Paul flattened himself on the ground and cautiously peered under the bush. Behind the tangled branches he could see the rough wall of the cliff, and in that wall a gaping, black hole. "There's a cave behind here!" he shouted.

They took turns to call Lula, but in vain. The hole in the cliff seemed to have swallowed her completely.

"We'll have to go in there," said Tania. "How can we get rid of this bush?" They attempted to snap the twigs, but they were tough, springy and covered with prickles. Paul tried the biggest blade of his pocket-knife, but he made little progress. "We need that axe of Dad's," he said, "and gloves for handling this stuff."

Just then there was a scraping, scrambling noise and Lula wriggled out from under the bushes. Tania grabbed her and hugged her, laughing with relief. They went back down the mountain, with Tania's belt threaded through Lula's collar.

"Shall we tell Mum and Dad about the cave?" asked Ellen.

"I'd sooner have a proper look at it first," said Paul. "We found it. We ought to have the first chance to explore it. Besides, it might be nothing much."

"I think it must go a long way back," said Tania, "or Lula would have come back sooner."

"We'll need a torch," said Jim. "We'll have to borrow Dad's big one. I know where he keeps it." He was delighted at the thought of using that torch. He was always borrowing it, switching it on and off, till someone scolded him for wasting the batteries.

"I'll take the axe tomorrow, when Dad's writing," said Paul.

"I'll borrow Mum's leather gloves," said Tania. "Our knitted ones wouldn't be any good against those prickles."

They were in such high spirits for the rest of the day that Mrs Blair was a bit suspicious. "I think the children are plotting something, William. They're in a strange, giddy mood. And they're not quarrelling. It just isn't normal!"

"It's the mountain air," said Mr Blair. "They're only enjoying themselves."

6 INSIDE THE CAVE

It took all Paul's strength to swing the axe. His arms and shoulders were soon aching badly. Tania looked on anxiously. "Do be careful. It's terribly sharp. If you hit your foot, you might cut it right off!"

"Stop fussing!" muttered Paul. "I know what I'm doing." He was not at all happy with the axe. He was frustrated by his lack of skill and hated the way the blade sometimes rebounded from the springy wood.

Ellen and Jim stood well clear, holding Lula's collar, watching eagerly. Each time a branch was cut off, Tania pulled it clear with her gloved hands.

At last there was a big enough gap in the thorny twigs. Paul leaned the axe against a boulder and wiped the sweat from his forehead. He had meant to be first to look inside the cave, but while he was getting his breath back, Jim quickly slipped past him. Holding the big torch with both hands,

Jim shone it into the gap in the cliff. Before Tania could stop him, he clambered inside. Lula leapt after him.

"Wait, Jim! Be careful!" shouted Paul. Tania switched on her little pocket torch and hurriedly followed her younger brother. She found herself in a tunnel sloping steeply downwards. The roof was low and covered with projections, and she could not stand upright.

"You stay out here, Ellen," ordered Paul, "just in case anything goes wrong. We'll give you a call if it's safe inside."

Ellen waited, fidgeting. What was she supposed to do if the others got into trouble? She had no ropes, no torch. She pictured herself running down the mountain, screaming for help. Then, to her relief, a shout came echoing up from the darkness. "Come on in, Ellen! It's all right."

The tunnel was short and widened to a small cavern. Paul snatched the big torch from Jim and shone it up at the roof. The children gasped. Above them hung a mass of pale cones, streaked with pink and orange.

"Stalactites!" said Tania excitedly. "See, Jim, they're formed by water, seeping through, dissolving the limestone. It's a really good cave!"

Paul lowered the torch beam. The walls glistened like the roof, covered with strange formations, columns and draperies.

"Look, more tunnels!" yelled Paul. He flashed the torch into the nearest dark opening, then stepped back quickly. Before his feet yawned a black hole. It looked very very deep. The torch light could not penetrate far into its depths. Tania picked up a pebble and tossed it down. They heard it bouncing far, far away, rebounding off the rocky walls. At last they thought they heard a faint splash.

"There's water down there," said Jim. He imagined himself tumbling into the shaft, falling and falling. He shuddered and backed away.

The children explored a second opening, treading cautiously, probing ahead of them with the torch. The tunnel sloped deep into the

mountain. The roof swooped up and down. The rocks glistened with moisture and the floor was slippery with mud. Then they came to a place where the tunnel divided into three forks.

"Which way shall we go?" whispered Ellen. She somehow felt the need to lower her voice in the caves.

"We'd better stop here," said Tania. "We might get lost. We need chalk to mark the walls, to help us find our way back."

"I suppose we could do with a rope too," said Paul reluctantly. "And more lights. And we'd better show Mum and Dad what we've found. Where's Lula?"

Lula appeared at the mouth of one of the

passages. "She seems to see in the dark better than we can," said Ellen.

They made their way back to the daylight and then rushed down the slopes to the house in high excitement. "Mum! Dad! We've found a cave!"

Mr and Mrs Blair were impressed when the children showed them the cave. They were also extremely angry. The children listened to the tirade in bewilderment.

"How could you go in there on your own!" cried Mrs Blair. "I thought you at least, Tania, had more sense! You might have slipped and fallen down one of those shafts. Potholing is a dangerous sport. It's for properly equipped adults, not scatterbrained children."

"I told you not to touch that axe," said Mr Blair to Paul.

"I don't think you did, Dad," said Paul, trying to remember exactly what his father had said on the subject. Mr Blair was not too certain either, and was annoyed with himself for not being sure.

"Well, you must have known you were not supposed to use it, or you would have asked me before you borrowed it."

"We wanted the cave to be a surprise," said Jim. "We thought you'd like it."

"We were very careful," said Ellen indignantly. She could not see why her parents were being so unreasonable.

Mrs Blair was examining her gloves. She was very cross. The palms were dull and scratched and there was a large tear in one of the thumbs. "These were expensive, Tania. You've ruined them."

"Sorry," said Tania. She had not realised the damage the thorns had inflicted on the gloves.

"Well, we'll say no more about it," said Mr Blair. "But you're to keep right away from here. It's just too risky. Caves like these need exploring and charting by experts. Show a bit of sense, all of you!"

The children marched soberly off downhill with their parents following more slowly. "How am I supposed to concentrate on my writing if I have to worry about what they might be doing all day?" Mr Blair asked his wife.

"It was you who bought a house in the mountains!" said Mrs Blair.

7 THE MYSTERIOUS BONES

They were high on the slopes when the storm broke. It had come suddenly, almost without warning. Dark clouds rolled in swiftly from the south and a faint flicker of lightning was followed by a slow roll of thunder. The house was in sight, but very far away.

The children started off downhill, but before long the rain began and they were soon drenched. The lightning became more frequent and the thunder louder.

Ellen grew very pale. She was afraid of storms. Jim, who was scared of many things, could laugh at thunder and lightning, but they made Ellen panic. She had no idea why. She stumbled along, her face as white as her socks, clutching Tania's hand and shaking all over. By the time they were halfway home, the others were worried about her.

"It's not far to the cave!" shouted Paul through the rain. "We'd better shelter there, while this passes." Tania opened her mouth to protest, then glanced at her sister and changed her mind.

"Come on, Ellen," she said. "We'll be there in no time."

They scrambled down the sloping tunnel into the blackness of the cavern. Luckily, Tania's little torch was in her pocket. Surprisingly, it worked. "Don't waste the battery," said Paul, when they were safe inside. "We might need it some other time."

They sat in the dark and talked. After a while their eyes became used to the blackness. A little daylight was filtering down the tunnel and they could just make out the rough outlines of the cave. They could barely hear the storm outside.

Time passed very slowly. "I'll see if it's any better now," said Tania. She picked her way up the tunnel to look. If anything the rain was heavier. Water was streaming down the cliff face and cascading over the mouth of the cave. But mostly it flowed off the ledge outside, and very little trickled back into the tunnel.

"It's still pouring!" said Tania, returning to the others. "It's a good job we came in here."

The children were feeling very cold in their wet clothes. Now and then a gust of wind blew down the tunnel and made them shiver. "It'll be warmer further inside," said Paul. "Give me the torch, Tania."

"We ought to stay here!" said Tania. "You know what Dad said."

"I won't go far," said Paul. "Just a few metres and we might be out of the draught." He avoided the tunnel with the yawning hole and the one they had explored the day before. The third opening was wide and low. He stooped down and cautiously stepped inside. With some anxiety, the others watched the flickering light of the torch disappear. But they did not have long to wait. Paul returned almost immediately.

"I've found something strange," he said. "Come and look! It's quite safe. There are no holes."

Eagerly the others followed him down a short, low passage. They found themselves in a larger cave. The ground was dry, the air felt slightly warmer. There were no stalactites on this roof, just overhanging rocks, fretted into huge, rounded hollows. "What's this thing you've found?" asked Ellen. "I can't see anything special."

"Over there, by the wall," said Paul, flashing the torch. "Bones!"

They hurried over to look. There were several bones scattered over the rocky ground, some of them astonishingly large. Ellen dropped on her knees and ran her fingers over the smooth, pale surface of one of the largest bones. "How did they get here?"

"Some animal must have crawled in here to die," said Tania.

"A long time ago," said Paul. "It must have been huge. Look at the size of this one! I think it's a thigh bone, but it's far too big for a horse or a cow." He slipped his hands under the great bone and tried to lift it. As it was surprisingly light, he suspected it might be hollow.

"Maybe it was a dinosaur!" said Jim, looking nervously into the shadows of the cave.

"Lots of the bones are missing," said Tania. "Perhaps other animals dragged them away."

Ellen scuffed her foot on the rock and felt something under her shoe. She picked it up – a hard, curved object, with a sharp point at one end. She rubbed the dust from it with her thumbs. In the feeble light of the torch it had the colour and sheen of bronze. "Look what I've found!"

"It's a claw, a huge claw!" said Tania, looking over her shoulder. "Don't you think so, Paul?"

Paul took the thing and turned it over and over. "That's what it looks like. I suppose it belonged to the same animal as the bones."

"Let me see," begged Jim. He stared hard at the claw. "It's from the thing that made my footprint. The one on the rock."

The children were silent for a minute. "It could be," said Tania cautiously. "But that was the print of a bird. Imagine a bird with legs as long as that! Whatever would it look like?"

They were still wondering as they climbed out of the cave and found that the storm had passed. The grass and rocks gleamed wet and a thin ray of sunlight slanted through the clouds. They had left the bones in the cave, but Ellen was carrying the claw.

"Don't show it to Mum and Dad," said Paul. "We'd have to explain where we found it."

8 LULA IS LOST

For several days Lula had had her run of the valley. Mostly she followed the children, but sometimes she wandered off on her own. Mr and Mrs Blair were relieved to have her away from the house. She always came home in the evening, at dinner time. It was the children's job to feed her, to open the tin of pet food and spoon meat out into her dish. Afterwards she settled down at the fireside as it was cold in the mountains after sunset.

But the day after the children found the bones in the cave, Lula did not return for her dinner. The food in the dish was untouched. The children went to bed, very unhappy. Next day they searched all over the valley, calling Lula's name, but they heard no answering bark, they found no clues. Their parents helped for a time, but without success. "Cheer up!" said Mr Blair. "It's no use worrying. She'll probably find her own way back."

But the children could not help worrying.

That night they shut themselves in one of the bedrooms, to talk things over.

"She might have gone right over the mountains," said Paul. "And we're supposed to stay in sight of the house!"

"She could have gone into the cave," said Ellen. "She may be lost in the dark, or perhaps she's fallen down a hole."

They sat and thought about it. "We just have to search in there!" said Tania. "But we daren't tell Mum and Dad. They've told us to keep out of the caves. And they're always getting cross with Lula. They'd blame her for the whole thing."

The others agreed. "We'd better be extra careful," said Ellen. "I'll find something to make marks on the rocks, so that we can find our way out again."

"We can't take Dad's torch – he might notice," said Paul. "How are your batteries, Tania?"

"Pretty feeble," replied Tania. "I don't think they'd last more than five minutes. I wish I'd brought some spares."

"We could take one of those," said Jim, nodding towards the candle perched on the chest of drawers.

"Better than nothing," said Paul. "But it would keep going out."

Tania suddenly remembered something. "Wait a minute," she said. "I can fix it." She stepped into the passage and closed the door softly behind her. She could hear her parents talking in the kitchen. Their bedroom door was open. She tiptoed quietly through it . . .

Five minutes later, looking very pleased with herself, she burst back into the room where the others were waiting. "It's all right," she said. "The torch works beautifully now. I swapped the batteries for those in the transistor radio. They're the same size."

"But now the radio won't work!" protested Paul. "Mum and Dad are going to be put out about that!"

"We have to find Lula," said Ellen. "That's more important than anything else."

They set off next morning, right after breakfast, carrying a picnic lunch in a string bag. "Take your parkas," said Mrs Blair. "The weather changes so quickly here. I don't want you soaked the way you were the other day."

The children grumbled, but they knotted the sleeves of the parkas around their waists.

Ellen had hidden a candle and matches in her pocket, in case they should need extra light in the cave. Jim's pockets were stuffed with biscuits to feed to Lula, if they found her. Paul had collected the rope from the car and carried it coiled over his shoulder. He thought it likely that they would need it. They made their way up the mountain to the cave.

"Make sure Mum isn't outside," said Tania. "She might spot us up here." The children gazed down at the little timber house. Nothing stirred in the valley. They knew their father's window faced in the other direction.

"Quick!" said Paul. "Into the cave!"

Inside, with only one small torch, it seemed darker than ever. The candle proved unmanageable, flickering and dropping hot wax. Tania played the tiny beam from the torch over the gleaming walls, marvelling at the strange and beautiful shapes of the rock.

"You'd better keep the light down by our feet," said Paul. "There are stalagmites to trip over."

"We're just as likely to bang our heads," replied his sister. "We'll have to move very slowly."

They shouted Lula's name through the three openings in the first chamber, then listened hard. The tunnels echoed faintly, but there was no reply. Then they shouted down the deep hole in the first tunnel. To their relief there was no answering whimper.

"The cave with the bones was a dead end," said Paul. "Let's try the other way."

Slowly, in single file, they crept along the tunnel, Tania in front with the torch. When they came to the place where the passage split into three, they paused while Paul scratched an arrow on the rocks, pointing back to the entrance. Ellen had found a reddish stone which made quite a good mark on the rocky wall.

They first tried the tunnel on the right, but after a few metres it ended in a pit, plunging down sheer between the rocks. The second passage was very narrow and after a little while the children found they could no longer squeeze through it.

"It's no use," complained Ellen. "We're not getting anywhere! We've been calling to Lula all the time. Surely if she's anywhere in the caves she'd have heard us!"

But the third tunnel looked more promising. The roof was high and most of the time the children could walk without stooping. On and on they went, the torchlight skimming the rough, muddy floor and damp, shining walls. Then, just as they were beginning to think there was no end to this winding passage, they saw a faint glow up ahead of them.

"I can see daylight!" cried Jim.

"I can smell fresh air," said Ellen. They paused and felt the feather of a breeze against their cheeks.

Paul funnelled his hands round his mouth and shouted, "Lula! Lula!" And away in the distance they heard a faint, answering bark.

9 SNOW IN SUMMER

The children stood at the tunnel mouth, blinking in the bright sunlight. Ahead of them the landscape was completely strange—even the rocks looked different. Unfamiliar ranges rose one behind the other. But it was the nearest mountain that caught their attention. It seemed to rise almost into the clouds, its peak glistening white against the blue sky.

"Snow!" cried Ellen. "That's snow up there, isn't it?"

Tania shaded her eyes with her hand. "I don't know," she said. "Could it be some sort of white rock?"

"No," said Paul in amazement. "It's snow all right."

"There's Lula!" shouted Jim, scrambling down the slope. The others stopped staring at the mountain and followed him.

The dog was lying under a small, scrubby tree. She had somehow managed to hook her collar onto

one of the branches. When she tried to pull loose, it threatened to throttle her. She looked up at the children, wagging her tail furiously.

"You clumsy old thing, Lula!" said Tania, falling on her knees to unbuckle the collar. "However did you manage that?"

"It's our fault," said Paul. "The collar must be too loose. Gosh, I bet she has a stiff neck!" He rubbed the dog gently behind the ears.

Jim pulled the biscuits from his pocket and fed them to Lula, who ate ravenously. To the children's relief she seemed none the worse for her experience. Happily they ate their own picnic lunch.

Tania sat on a small boulder and gazed up at the strange mountain. "It's the place where the snow never melts," she said. "Remember what the old lady in the store told us? She used to look for it year after year! And we've found it just by accident!"

"Lula found it," said Paul, patting the dog. "And we found Lula."

"Let's go up there," said Ellen suddenly. "I've never seen snow and neither has Jim. It wouldn't take long."

"We ought to get back," said Tania. "We were not supposed to even go out of sight of the house. We were told to keep out of the caves."

"But we've done all that already," said Ellen.

"We couldn't help it. We had to find Lula. Now that we're here, surely it wouldn't matter if we had a look at the snow. I want to touch it with my fingers. I want to make a snowball."

Paul looked at his watch. "It's early," he said, "and the slopes on this side look easy. We could be up and down pretty quickly, Tania."

"Well, I don't want to go!" said Jim.

"Why ever not?" Paul, Tania and Ellen looked at him in surprise.

"You've forgotten about the monsters," said Jim. "That old woman said there were monsters!"

The others started to laugh. "Don't be silly, Jim!" said Tania. "She didn't say that exactly. That was only an old story. I promise there won't be any monsters."

"I still don't want to go," said Jim. But his brother and sisters hustled him along with them. They could not leave him on his own, and by now they were determined to climb up to the snow. Lula followed, not very eagerly, but unwilling to let the children out of her sight.

The higher they climbed, the colder it grew. They were glad of the parkas they had wanted to leave at home. They toiled up the slopes for a long while. The peak was not as close as it had seemed from down below. From time to time Paul glanced behind them, careful to keep the dark splotch of the tunnel mouth in view. It would be disastrous to lose their way. The vegetation grew sparser and sparser and soon they were walking over bare rock.

A short way from the top, where the mountain towered higher than any of its neighbours, they were suddenly hit by a freezing wind and the rock became slippery with ice. Tania started to wish that they had not come. Jim was too cold and miserable to worry about monsters. They stumbled on towards the peak with watery eyes and chattering teeth.

And at last they were there, high on the roof of the world, up to their ankles in fine, powdery snow. Ellen snatched a handful and threw it at Tania. Tania rolled a snowball and flung it back. It missed Ellen and broke against Paul's shoulder. Jim forgot his worries and joined in. They were soon breathless with laughter. They pelted each other with snow, forgetting their blue fingers and painfully cold feet. Lula jumped round them, barking with excitement.

"We mustn't stay long," said Tania at last, grabbing Paul's wrist to look at his watch.

"Enough's enough!" said Paul. "My toes are going to drop off."

Just at that moment a snowball from Ellen hit him full in the face. Paul gasped and shook his head, then started to chase his sister. Laughing, Ellen darted away over the snow. And then, with a small scream, she disappeared.

10 ELLEN MAKES A DISCOVERY

The others stood for a moment, stiff with fright, then began to run towards the spot where she had disappeared. Ellen must have fallen into a crevice. They thought of the deep, dark shafts in the cave. Perhaps she had fallen hundreds of metres. She might have broken a leg. She might be dead! On their hands and knees they peered desperately into the jagged hole in the snow. Then, to their relief, they heard her voice.

"I've fallen down a sort of crack!"

"Can you climb out?" shouted Paul.

"I think so," called Ellen. "There seem to be a lot of footholds." The others waited uneasily. Lula crouched in the snow beside them and whined.

Ellen looked around her. She was standing in a deep cleft, dimly lit by the gaping hole overhead. The ground beneath her was glassy and the rocks on either side glittered with icicles. Directly beneath the hole was a drift of new snow.

Cautiously exploring the rocks with her hands and feet, Ellen began to climb up towards the daylight. She was about halfway when her foot slipped on a patch of ice and shot from under her. She kicked wildly, dislodging several small rocks, and fell backwards, down into the snowdrift. She scrambled to her feet again, shaken but unhurt apart from a bruised knee.

"What's happening?" called Tania. "Are you all right?"

"I fell down again," shouted Ellen. "It's slippery and some of the rocks are loose."

Paul suddenly remembered the rope. "Wait a minute! I'll get the rope, Ellen."

As Ellen stood waiting, something caught her eye—something gleaming in the snow amongst the fallen rocks. It was a stone, the size of a man's head, smooth, round and a deep, glowing red. In the shaft of daylight it flickered with bronze shadows. Ellen almost forgot her plight. She brushed aside the snow with her numb fingers and scooped up the strange rock. It was heavy, but not as heavy as she expected.

The end of the rope snaked down and tapped her on the shoulder.

"Hey!" shouted Ellen. "I've found the most marvellous stone! You should see it!"

"Stop playing around down there, Ellen," scolded Tania. "Tie the rope round your waist and we'll help to pull you out."

Ellen replaced the stone on the snow. She could not bear to leave it behind, but she knew she would need both of her hands to climb out of the crack. With a sudden inspiration she tightened the strings of the parka around her waist.

She unzipped the front of the jacket and slipped the stone inside, then pulled up the zip, feeling the stone's iciness against her chest. She tied the rope round her waist.

"Hurry up, Ellen! What are you doing down there?" shouted Paul.

"I'm ready," called Ellen. "Start pulling!" Minutes later she was back with the others, on top of the mountain.

"Are you all right, Ellen? Why are you bending over like that?"

Ellen fell on her knees and unzipped her parka. She rolled the icy lump out onto the snow and sighed with relief. "Look at this rock I found! Isn't it beautiful?"

Lula sniffed the rock and growled softly. The hair stood up all along her back.

"It's not a rock!" said Tania in surprise, pulling Lula away. It's an egg!"

"An egg?" said Paul scornfully. "Don't be silly!" Then he stopped. The thing was certainly shaped like an egg. Its surface was smooth and, now that he looked at it closely, more like a shell than a stone.

"Whoever heard of an egg that colour?" he said uncertainly.

"Whoever heard of an egg that size?" said Jim.

"All the same," said Tania, "it *is* an egg, a huge red egg, and it's frozen solid. It must be something very rare. How can we carry it?"

"Not inside my parka again," said Ellen. "My front feels frozen."

Paul picked up the string bag that had held the picnic lunch and stuffed the sandwich wrappings into his pockets. "I'll hold it open. See if the egg will go in." Tania picked up the egg with tingling fingers. She manoeuvred it into the bag.

They hurried back down the mountain, eager for the warmth of the lower slopes. Paul and Tania swung the egg between them. We won't be able to show it to Mum and Dad," said Paul. "We'd have to explain where we found it."

"We'd better not say where we found Lula," said Tania. "They would be cross with her, as well as with us."

That night they sat whispering in the girls' bedroom. The strange egg glowed like a great ruby in the flickering candlelight.

"It isn't the egg of any bird alive today," said Tania. "It belonged to some creature that died out a long time ago."

"Ages ago," said Paul. "Perhaps hundreds of years."

"It must have a strong shell," said Ellen. "It didn't break when it froze. When we put those eggs in the freezer last year, all the shells split."

"A different sort of shell," said Paul. "A different sort of egg, laid by a very different sort of bird!"

"It must have been enormous," said Ellen. "As big as the one that made the footprint on the rock."

"As big as the thing that left the bones in the cave," said Jim.

"Could they all have come from the same creature?" asked Tania. They gazed at the egg and wondered.

Jim reached out and stroked it gingerly. "What if it hatches?" The others spluttered with laughter.

"Eggs don't hatch when they've been frozen," said Tania.

"Especially when they've been frozen as long as this one," said Paul. "Don't be an idiot, Jim."

Jim scowled at his brother. "How do you know? You don't know anything at all about this sort of egg!" He had raised his voice.

Tania was afraid her mother and father might hear. "Ssh," she whispered. "Where are we going to keep it?"

"Under my bed," gloated Ellen. "It's mine really. I found it! I've made it a little nest." She pulled a cardboard box, full of crumpled newspaper, from under the bed.

"I don't see that it's yours," objected Paul. "We all helped. You'd never have found it on your own."

"It was Lula who found the place where the snow never melts," said Tania. "It was Paul and I who carried the egg all the way home."

"Ellen, all *you* did was to fall down a hole," said Jim.

"And if I hadn't taken the rope," said Paul, "you'd still be down there."

"It is so mine!" hissed Ellen. "All right, all right! See if I care!" She hoped she wasn't going to cry. "Where d'you want to keep it then?"

There was a moment's silence.

"Come to think of it," said Paul, "under Ellen's bed is about the best place. There's no room under Jim's. Dad's stuffed all sorts of junk there."

"I suppose it might be a good idea," said Tania, who, like Paul, slept on one of the air-beds. "Mum leaves the cleaning in here to us. She's not likely to poke around."

Jim lifted the egg and placed it gently in the box. Ellen rearranged the newspaper to hide it. Then, triumphantly, she slid the box right under her bed, against the warm kitchen wall.

And there it lay for nearly a week. From time to time, one of the children pulled out the box and peeped at the egg, glowing among the creased newspapers. They marvelled at its size and its colour, then pushed it back again into its hiding place.

11 THE ACCIDENT

The weather grew suddenly colder.

"Whatever happened to summer?" groaned Mrs Blair one afternoon as she looked up at the gloomy sky. "I hope the rest of our holiday won't be like this! I wish we could hear a weather forecast, but there's something wrong with that transistor radio."

"It's going to be cold tonight all right," muttered Mr Blair, swinging his axe. "Lucky we've plenty of wood!" He was proud of his growing skill. Firewood was stacked by the kitchen hearth and a neat pile of logs was rising outside the door.

The children stood well clear, watching their father wield the axe. The blade bit deep into the logs and branches, and sharp, clean, white chips of wood flew far and wide.

How the accident happened, no one was exactly sure. Perhaps the axe hit a very hard knot. Perhaps Mr Blair stumbled and lost his balance. He blamed Lula, who dashed past suddenly, barking at a lizard. At any event, the blade glanced off a springy branch and gashed Mr Blair's leg. It began to bleed very fast.

Mrs Blair ran to find a towel and a basin of water. She hastily cleaned the leg, then held a compress over the wound. At last the bleeding stopped.

"It's going to need stitching," said Paul, peering at the gash. "That was awfully bad luck, Dad!"

"You could do with a tetanus shot too," said Mrs Blair. "I'll have to drive you down to a doctor. Keep still, William! You don't want to start the bleeding again. I'll get the car ready. Paul, find your father's jacket. He's shivering."

Mr Blair sat on the grass, looking very pale, with his leg sticking straight out in front of him. "Carefully now," said his wife. "You'd better sit in the back. Then you can prop up your leg on the seat."

"How about the children?" asked Mr Blair.

Mrs Blair frowned. "They'll have to stay here. It will take us a long time to drive to the doctor and back. Ellen and Jim are too young to be up half the night. Tania, Paul, I'm relying on you to look after the others. Make sure Ellen cleans her teeth. Don't let Jim help with the cooking; he's a menace with that open fire. We'll get back as soon as we can."

"We'll be all right," said Tania. "How does the leg feel, Dad?"

"Just throbbing a bit," said Mr Blair. "I'll be fine again in no time."

They drove slowly away, Mrs Blair anxious not to hit bumps or potholes. She thought that a sudden jolt might restart the bleeding. The children watched the car disappear, then went into the house.

"It's getting colder and colder," said Tania. "The bedrooms are going to be freezing. I wish we had some extra blankets."

"I'll build up the fire tonight," said Paul. "If we leave the doors open, the warmth should flow right round the house."

They did not think about dinner until it was getting dark outside. There was soup in the largest pan, left over from the night before, and it seemed to be enough for four. Tania set it on one of the trivets to heat. At the other side of the fireplace she fried bacon in a pan that was growing blacker every day. Ellen toasted slices of bread, speared on the carving fork, trying not to get in Tania's way. Paul fed Lula outside and gave her fresh drinking water.

"Do you know," he said, coming in with the dog, "it's trying to snow out there!"

"It couldn't be," said Tania, turning the slices of bacon. "It's too early for snow."

Jim, who was laying the table, dropped the forks with a clatter and ran first to the window, where he could see very little, and then to the door. Ellen propped her toast on a plate in the hearth and followed him.

They returned triumphant. "What's that then?" asked Jim proudly, holding out his arm to Tania. Two tiny, white flakes were melting on his navy jumper.

"It looks like snow," admitted Tania, "but don't get excited. It probably won't settle. Remember what the shopkeeper said. No chance of snow for another three months at least."

"She doesn't know everything," said Ellen.

All through the meal, Jim and Ellen kept jumping up to peer out of the window into the darkness. They fancied they could see whirling snowflakes—perhaps they could. When Tania went to the door afterwards to throw away the tea-leaves, a snow-laden wind gusted into the hall. "The ground is white already!" she said in surprise. "We might be able to make snowballs tomorrow."

Paul brought extra wood into the kitchen. The little logs were sprinkled with snow, and hissed when he put them on the fire. Outside, the snow fell thicker and thicker, but it was cosy in the little house. The warmth of the fire spread to every corner, even to where the strange egg lay in its nest of newspapers, under Ellen's bed.

Ellen and Jim went to bed early. They wanted to make the morning come faster—a morning when they planned to have a snow fight, make a snowman, perhaps even use a tray as a toboggan.

By the kitchen fire, Paul and Tania talked softly. "Mum and Dad won't be able to get back up the road," said Paul. "We're going to be snowed up."

"It won't last long," said Tania. "Not at this time of the year. And we've plenty of firewood and food."

Later they fastened the old, black spark-guard in front of the fire and went off to bed. Lula slumbered heavily on the kitchen rug. For a while all was dark and quiet.

12 THE HATCHING

Ellen woke suddenly in the middle of the night and lay quietly, listening. From somewhere quite near, she could hear a tiny noise—a scratching, a tapping, too gentle for Lula, too loud for a beetle. Mice? she thought, or could it be a rat? She liked mice, but rats were another matter.

The noise came again. It was underneath her—right under the bed! What if a big rat with red eyes was gnawing her bedroom slippers?

With a bound Ellen was out of bed and across the room. Tania lay curled up in a sleeping-bag on her lilo. Ellen shook her by the shoulder. "Tania, wake up! Wake up! There's something under my bed!"

Yawning, Tania sat up and lit the candle. She tried to be patient. Jim often had nightmares, but Ellen usually slept very soundly. "What sort of something?"

"I thought it might be a rat," said Ellen, cheered by the light and her sister's support.

65

"I hope not!" said Tania. She carried the candle across the room and set it on the floor. Together they peeped under the bed. There was nothing new there, just Ellen's slippers, quite ungnawed, and the old cardboard box, pushed back against the kitchen wall.

"You were dreaming!" said Tania, then stopped. She heard the noise herself. "It's coming from the box," she said.

"What's the matter?" called Paul, from across the passage.

"There's something under my bed!" shouted Ellen. Paul stumbled sleepily into the room, with Jim close behind him.

"It's probably only a mouse," said Tania. "Something's climbed in there, among the newspapers. If you keep very quiet, you'll hear it." While Paul and Jim listened on their hands and knees, she fetched a broom from the kitchen. She slid it under Ellen's bed and pushed the cardboard box out into the middle of the floor. "It might be a snake!" said Jim. "Or a big black spider!"

Tania stood grasping the broom, ready if necessary to hit anything that appeared. Paul tweaked away one piece of newspaper, then another. Then suddenly he stopped. He leaned over the box, staring as if he couldn't believe his eyes. "Good grief!"

"What is it?" gasped Ellen.

"The egg! The noise is coming from the egg! And there's a crack in it. Come and look!"

Incredulously the others gazed and listened. It was quite true. The tapping and scraping came from inside the shell, and across the shiny, red surface of the egg ran a dark, crooked line.

"It's hatching!" cried Jim. "You said it wouldn't! You said it couldn't!" Paul, Tania and Ellen watched, shocked into silence. A tiny hole appeared in the middle of the crack. Then the creature inside seemed to rest for a while. By now the children were shivering.

"We can't go back to bed while this is happening," said Tania. "Let's take it into the kitchen. It's warmer in there." She and Paul held the box gingerly, at arm's length. They carried it carefully into the kitchen and set it down on the rug in front of the fire.

Lula growled menacingly.

"We'd better shut her out," said Ellen. She grabbed the dog, pushed her into the passage, and closed the door.

The fire had died down, but it was still warm in the kitchen. Tania poked fresh wood into the embers and the flames blazed up. The children sat with blankets round their shoulders, eagerly watching the egg. The baby inside was active again, tapping and scratching. The egg rocked slightly in its newspaper nest.

"D'you think we should help it?" asked Paul. "Should we break the shell?"

"Better not," said Tania. "Not unless it's really in trouble. We might hurt it."

"It should be a beautiful bird," said Ellen, "coming from such a beautiful egg!"

The hole was a little larger now. A tiny piece of the shell fell away and something poked through the opening. "Is that its beak?" asked Ellen breathlessly. But it was not a beak. It was a tiny claw.

"I thought birds pecked their way out of shells," said Tania. "I didn't know they broke them with their feet."

The claw disappeared. Something red and shiny showed for a moment in the opening, then quickly vanished. The scratching began again. "I saw its eye," cried Jim. "It looked at me!"

After that, things happened faster. New cracks appeared, more pieces of shell fell away. The tapping grew in a frantic crescendo. As they caught fresh glimpses of what was in the egg, the children's eyes grew wider and wider. At last an exhausted little creature heaved itself from the shell and lay panting in the newspapers.

"What is it?" cried Tania. "Some sort of lizard?"

The long, sinuous body was covered with

scales, mostly green, but shading to yellow on the belly and under the barbed tail. A row of five pointed spurs ran down the spine. The creature had only two legs, thick and short, ending in clawed feet, like those of an eagle. The snout was long, with flaring nostrils. The eyes glittered red. On top of its head were knobs that looked like budding horns.

Ellen leaned closer to look. "It's a dragon," she said softly.

"Yes," agreed Jim. "That's what it is."

"It can't be!" said Paul. "Dragons are mythical. They only happen in legends."

"Well, what is this then?" asked Tania. "Look at those things folded along its sides. I think they're wings."

As if it heard her, the little creature stretched. The wings unfurled, ribbed like the wings of a bat, green on the upper side, yellow beneath. They did not look big enough for flying, but Jim backed away nervously.

Paul felt dazed. What could the thing be? The scales of a fish, the body of a reptile, the wings of a bat, the claws of a bird. He decided he was dreaming. "All right," he said. "It's a dragon."

The dragon's wings were folded again. It lay wearily in the box, its big, hooded eyelids closed. "He needs to sleep," said Tania. "He's tired after

breaking out of the shell."

For a long time they watched the dragon, but it did not move. They began to feel very tired themselves. Jim could hardly keep his eyes open. "We'd better go back to bed," said Tania. "He'll be safe, here in the kitchen."

When they opened the door, Lula bounded

in, growling. They hastily pulled her away from the box. "It's all right, Lula," said Paul. "He's a nice dragon. He's only a baby."

The dog seemed unconvinced, so they were forced to shut her out in the passage again for the rest of the night.

13 KEEPING THE SECRET

Paul woke up and stretched on his air-bed. "I had a weird dream. A dragon hatched out of that egg!"

Jim jumped out of bed. "It wasn't a dream," he said. "It was real."

They hurried to the kitchen. The girls were already there, squatting on the floor, watching what was happening inside the cardboard box. There was a steady crunching noise. The little dragon was eating the shell, his sharp teeth grinding it up with surprising ease.

Tania held Lula's collar firmly and stroked her head. The dog was calmer than she had been the night before. From time to time she whined uneasily, but she did not struggle to break loose to attack the dragon. "I'm training them to be friends," said Tania.

Paul looked doubtful. "You can train dogs all right," he said, "but how do you know you can train a dragon?"

"I don't see why not," said Ellen, hanging over the box. "People have all sorts of strange pets—monkeys, cheetahs, sometimes even lions!" Before anyone could stop her, she reached out her hand and tickled the dragon between his budding horns. The little animal froze, then he half closed his eyes with a blissful expression. A faint rumble arose from the box, remarkably like a purr.

"There, you see!" said Ellen. "He's as tame as anything already. Now what shall I call him?"

"Why should *you* choose? Why can't *I* pick his name?" cried Jim.

"I bet I can think of better names than either of you," said Paul.

"He's my dragon," shouted Ellen. "I found the egg. He belongs to me. I'm going to name him!"

Tania exploded. "Ellen, we're not starting all that again. Stop it this minute, or I'll thump you! We want to choose the best possible name, so we need ideas from everyone."

Ellen sulked and refused to join in. The others took a long time to decide. Tania insisted that a dragon, even such a small one, should have a hot and splendid name. They argued over "Firelord", "Brimstone" and "Fireball". At last they decided on "Firedrake." Paul said it was a very old name for a dragon.

"Take no notice!" whispered Ellen, into the box. "Your real name is Zoom!"

Tania mixed up some powdered milk, warmed

it in a pan and offered it to Firedrake-Zoom. He lapped it eagerly with his barbed tongue, then settled back to sleep. The children sat down to their own breakfast. The snowfall was over. Light, reflected from the white world outside, poured into the kitchen. In the excitement of the hatching, they had almost forgotten the snow. Now it gleamed enticingly through the window. Ellen and Jim gulped their cereal quickly, impatient to go outside.

"Why are you looking so glum, Tania?" asked Ellen.

"Mum and Dad will never let us keep him," said Tania, nodding towards Firedrake, asleep in his cardboard box. "They don't really enjoy having a dog. Lula is always getting into trouble. A dragon would be too much for them. Think of the way he ate that shell! If he chewed a slipper, there wouldn't be much left!"

"But we have to keep him!" cried Jim.

"We'll train him," said Ellen. "I know he'll learn quickly. He has clever eyes."

"We won't get the chance," said Paul. "You're right, Tania. They'll never agree to have him as a pet. And if anyone else hears we have a dragon, we'll lose him right away. This must be the only one in the world. Zoos will want him, scientists will chase him. Our only chance is to keep him a secret."

"But we can't," said Tania, "not in this little house. And soon we'll be going back home. What shall we do then?"

They went outside to look at the snow. Several inches lay crisp on the grass, and in places there were deeper drifts. Paul plodded along to take a look at the road. He did not think his parents would be able to get through.

Lula bounded about, leaving black paw marks in the snow. Ellen and Jim were building a snowman. Tania hunted for suitable pebbles for eyes and buttons.

They spent most of the morning outside, building, fighting and sliding. From time to time they ran to peep through the kitchen window at the sleeping dragon. By lunchtime they were wet, cold and ready to spend the rest of the day indoors.

The dragon was awake. He had managed to scramble out of his box and was roaming around the kitchen, red eyes glittering, claws scraping on the floorboards. From his snout to the barb at the end of his tail, he measured half a metre. Already he moved quickly and easily, snaking his tail quickly between the chairs, spinning round nimbly to gaze up at the children. He seemed very friendly, rubbing his scaly back against their legs, nuzzling their ankles. His breath was uncomfortably hot.

The children had no idea how to feed a

dragon. Milk seemed a bit inadequate, even if he was a baby. They offered him some of Lula's dog food and he ate it readily, polishing the dish with a rapidly flickering tongue.

Lula watched the new pet warily, but made no more threatening noises. When he slept on the hearthrug in the evening, she edged nearer and nearer, anxious not to miss her share of the fire.

"How big d'you think he'll grow?" asked Jim, stroking the little green head.

"Oh, pretty big," said Paul, vaguely remembering rather alarming stories about dragons. "But that'll take ages. We don't need to worry about it yet."

"We do have to worry about Mum and Dad," said Tania. "I can't see how we'll hide him, once they get back."

"Perhaps the snow will go on and on," said Ellen dreamily. "Perhaps they won't get back for months and months."

But when they woke next morning there was a thaw. And at midday the Blairs' car appeared over the rise and stopped outside the little house.

Mr Blair looked very pale as he limped into the hall. The first thing he saw was Lula, with a notebook dangling from her mouth. His shout of rage echoed to every corner of the house and brought the children scurrying through doorways.

"You've let that wretched dog into my room,"

he roared. "She's been chewing up my notes!" He launched himself towards Lula, then stopped, wincing from the pain in his leg. Paul pounced on the dog and retrieved the notebook.

"It's all right, honestly, Dad. She hasn't chewed it at all."

Mrs Blair came in, carrying bags and bundles of shopping, exhausted after the long drive. "Thank goodness that's over! We were so worried about you all when the snow started."

As soon as they could, the children slipped away. "Where's Firedrake?" whispered Paul.

"Under Ellen's bed," said Tania. "When we heard Dad shouting at Lula in the hall, he shot straight under there. I've shut the door. He can't get out."

That solved the problem for the moment. In the evening, Ellen sneaked a saucer of food into the bedroom. She lifted the bedspread and peeped under the bed. Two little red lights stared at her from the furthest corner. She pushed the saucer towards them. "Zoom . . . Zoom . . . Here's your dinner, little Zoom."

14 A VISIT FROM WALLY

Next day was fine, but the children did not dare to leave the house. They were afraid their parents might find Firedrake.

"I must mend that rip in Ellen's skirt," said Mrs Blair. "I'll do it now, while I think of it." She started to get up from her chair.

"I'll get it, Mum," said Tania, hurrying out of the door. She came back very quickly, the skirt in her hand.

"And I meant to darn that hole in Tania's sock," said Mrs Blair.

"I know where it is," said Ellen, scurrying into the passage.

Mrs Blair looked rather surprised. "Everyone's very helpful this morning," she said. "But why are you all indoors? It's a lovely day."

"It's a bit cold out there," said Paul. "We thought we'd sooner stay by the fire."

"Nonsense!" said his father, poking his head

round the door. "What a lot of namby-pamby creatures! Put on your warm jackets. How can I write with four children squabbling around the place?"

"We're not squabbling," protested Tania. "We're being very good and quiet. Can't we stay in, Dad? Please!"

"No, you can't," snapped Mr Blair, whose sore leg made him bad-tempered. "All that fine mountain air out there is going to waste. Go out and breathe some of it. Why d'you think we brought you up here?"

Just at that moment, Lula began to bark. Then there came a loud knock on the door. "Who on earth can that be?" wondered Mrs Blair. "I never thought we'd have visitors up here!"

"I have a horrible suspicion," said her husband.

Paul crossed to the window and looked out. "Whoops!" he said. "It's Mad Wally. Shotgun and all!"

"I thought so," said Mr Blair. "Marvellous! Just what I need this morning!" He limped away to open the front door. The children crowded into the passage behind him.

"Good morning," said Mad Wally, trying to step inside.

"Good morning," grunted Mr Blair grimly, blocking the doorway.

"I was asleep when you happened to drive past

yesterday," said Mad Wally.

"I know," said Mr Blair. "We could hear you snoring."

"You undid the chain without my permission," said Mad Wally reproachfully.

"So we did," said Mr Blair.

"By the time I woke up and came outside, you were away up the road."

"Well?" asked Mr Blair.

"So I asked myself," said Wally sternly, "why should anyone sneak past like that? And what was the answer? They were probably smuggling a cat! Maybe more than one cat!"

"Maybe forty cats," giggled Ellen, feeling brave behind her father's back.

"Forty cats?" bellowed Wally. "Did that child say forty cats?"

Mr Blair turned to glare at Ellen, then spun around again to Wally. "She's just being silly!" he shouted. "Have some sense, man. Whatever would we want with forty cats? We don't have any cats at all."

Mrs Blair hurried into the passage and whispered into her husband's ear. "Don't annoy him. He might be dangerous."

"Would you like a cup of tea, Mr Crumthorpe?" she asked. "The kettle's just coming to the boil."

Wally seemed pleased at the suggestion. He

propped his gun by the door and pulled off his woolly hat, revealing a scalp as bare and brown as an egg. He stood by the fire, sipping a steaming cup. His clothes were steaming too. It was probably damp in the house under the stone.

"How did you get here?" asked Tania, who could see no vehicle outside the window.

"I drove up in my truck," answered Wally, blowing on the liquid in his cup to cool it. "I left it down below the rise. When you're after cats, its best to creep up on them quietly."

Mrs Blair took a deep breath. "I'm sorry you went to so much trouble, Mr Crumthorpe. We've no cats here."

Mad Wally finished his tea and put down the cup on the table. "Well, since I'm here," he said, "you won't mind if I just check around?"

"We do mind!" snapped Mr Blair.

"And I ask myself . . . now *why* do you mind?" said Wally. "This begins to look very suspicious."

"Oh, let him look!" whispered Mrs Blair. "It's the quickest way to get rid of him."

The children looked at each other in alarm. While Wally was poking behind the kitchen sofa, they slipped away to the girls' bedroom. Firedrake pranced out from under the bed and frolicked around their ankles. "Where can we hide you, Zoom?" asked Ellen desperately. "If Wally's so fierce with cats, he'll hate dragons!"

Loud footsteps sounded outside the door. The handle turned. Tania pushed Firedrake out of sight, beneath the dangling bedspread.

Mad Wally stood holding his gun, looking around the little room. He gave three loud sniffs. "Sometimes," he said, "you can smell cats. They may keep quiet, but you can smell them out."

"I can't," said Jim.

"I've had a lot of practice," said Wally. "And you can hear them too. Not all cats are pussy-footed."

From under the bed came a little rasping sound; the sound of dragon claws skittering on floorboards.

"What have we here?" roared Wally. He leapt across the room and jerked the bedspread high in the air. Firedrake streaked out from under the bed, tripping up the old man. As Wally fell, his gun went off, shattering the window. The little dragon flashed through the doorway, down the passage and out of the open front door. Mrs Blair had left it ajar for a moment while she collected a fresh armful of logs for the fire. Bending over the woodpile, she saw nothing.

Mr Blair dashed for the bedroom as fast as his wounded leg would allow. He glared at the broken windowpane, then at Wally, who sprawled on the floor looking dazed. "What are you doing, you lunatic?" he shouted.

"A goanna!" said Wally. "I was tripped up by a goanna! These brats of yours were keeping a goanna under the bed! Don't you know that's not allowed?"

"How about my window?" asked Mr Blair fiercely. "I shall expect you to pay for that. Good grief, man! You might have hit the children with your wretched gun. Get out of here before I lose my temper."

Wally seemed shaken. He left the house without attempting to search the other rooms.

"What on earth was he talking about?" fumed Mr Blair, as he nailed a piece of board over the broken window. "A goanna? Nonsense of course! You didn't have a goanna in here did you, Tania?"

"No, Dad," said Tania truthfully. "We didn't have a goanna."

Ellen found the dragon hiding behind the woodpile and smuggled him back into the bedroom.

15 TIME TO GO HOME

Later the children whispered together, wondering what to do. "He can't stay in the bedroom for long," said Tania. "Sooner or later, Dad and Mum are bound to find him."

"We could keep him in the caves," suggested Jim. The others protested. "It's too dark in there. It's too damp, too big, too dangerous. He might fall down one of those holes."

"But perhaps we could find Zoom another cave," said Ellen. "A nice, light, comfortable, dry, little one."

"I wish you'd stop calling him that silly name," said Tania, "but it isn't a bad idea."

Next morning Paul and Tania went out to hunt for a suitable cave. Ellen and Jim were ordered to stand guard in the house. "Keep Mum and Dad out of that bedroom, whatever you do. If they see Firedrake, it'll ruin everything."

Luckily Mr and Mrs Blair were busy elsewhere. When Tania and Paul came home several hours later, the dragon was still a secret.

They smuggled him up the mountain in a shopping bag. The new cave was high on the ridge behind the house. It was very small, but a good, dry shelter. They had brought a dish and a bottle of drinking water. Paul balanced the dish in a corner of the cave and filled it to the brim. Ellen made Firedrake a bed with her oldest pullover.

The children built a low barrier of stones and branches across the mouth of the cave, to keep the dragon inside. He watched through a crack as they set off down the mountain.

Every day the children visited Firedrake. They put him on Lula's leash and took him for walks, high on the mountain. They had to make an extra hole in the collar, to keep it on his tiny neck. The dragon did not seem to mind the leash. He frisked along, exploring as eagerly as the dog, now and then flapping his small, useless wings and snorting with excitement.

"I was so sure I'd brought enough dog food!" said Mrs Blair one night, peering into the cupboard. "But at this rate it isn't going to last! Lula will have to eat a little less."

After that the children did not dare to take the pet food. They saved titbits from their own meals and smuggled them up the mountain. Firedrake seemed to like everything, even lumps of cheese. On walks he crunched up small, prickly plants. Once he pounced on a lizard, and before the children could blink, it was down his throat.

"He's learning to hunt!" said Ellen proudly.

"He's not very good at it yet," said Paul, as the dragon snapped unsuccessfully at a butterfly.

Lula was by now completely used to Firedrake. The children tried hard not to make her jealous. When they fussed over the dragon, they also remembered to pat the dog.

They were enthralled by their new pet — his strange, sinuous movements, his gleaming, red eyes, his shining bronze claws, the funny little roaring noise he made when he was over-excited.

When he nuzzled their hands or their ankles, his breath was a little too hot to bear. But he soon realised this and did not puff on their unprotected skins.

"What if he starts breathing fire?" asked Jim nervously.

Paul hooted with laughter. "Breathing fire! Don't be ridiculous."

The children had one great worry: they were going home very soon — how would Firedrake survive without them?

"He'll never catch enough lizards and things," said Tania. "He just isn't good enough yet. And he has no mother to look after him. We can't leave him up here alone."

"He'd be fine in the backyard at home," said Paul. "If we could only get him there."

The children sat thinking. The garden at home was long and narrow, surrounded by high fences. Mr and Mrs Blair hated gardening. They mowed the lawn at the front of the house, and a small patch by the kitchen door where the clothes hoist spun in the wind, but most of the back garden was a wilderness—a tangle of trees, shrubs and long, seeding grasses. What was more, you could close it off. A long time ago, someone had planted an orchard there and enclosed it with a wall. The children often ran in and out of the wild garden. The gate in the wall was always open—but it could be closed and fastened.

The more they thought about it, the better the idea seemed. Their parents hardly ever went through that gate. They preferred to forget the weeds and the unpruned trees behind it. Firedrake would be able to roam unnoticed in the undergrowth. The children could easily slip in there to feed him.

"But how can we get him home with us?" asked Jim.

Paul looked at the little creature basking in the sun. A daisy in front of his nostrils was slowly wilting and dipping over. "He's growing," he said, "but he's still not very big. Maybe we could sneak him into the car."

"Mum and Dad would be bound to notice," objected Tania.

"Not if he was in a box, or a bag. I was thinking about my sports bag. But what would I do with my clothes? I can't leave them all behind."

"We could put them in a plastic garbage bag," said Tania, "and tuck them into the trailer. Mum packs the towels that way."

"Will Zoom have enough air to breathe, inside the bag?" worried Ellen.

"I think there are a few eyelets," said Paul. "But I'll leave the zip a tiny bit open too. He'll be all right."

The Blairs were ready to leave the house in the mountains. The grate was cold and empty, the windows were fastened tight, and Mrs Blair had turned off the water.

"Come on, kids!" called Mr Blair. "What's keeping you? I want to lock the door." He stood jingling the keys impatiently.

The children came guiltily out of the house. Paul was carrying his sports bag and staggering slightly. Firedrake was getting rather heavy.

"Oh, Paul, really!" cried his mother. "That bag should have been with the rest of the cases." She looked at the trailer in dismay. It was tightly packed, the cover tied down with far more knots than usual. The children had made sure of that.

"Don't worry, Mum," said Tania. "We'll take it in the back with us. There's lots of room."

The children scrambled into the station wagon. Lula leapt in beside them. They positioned the bag right by the back window, as far away as possible from their parents. They were hoping that Firedrake would sleep for most of the journey, in the dark bag, lulled by the motion of the car. Lula sniffed at the bag and settled comfortably beside it.

Mr Blair started the engine. The dragon was startled by the unfamiliar noise. A faint roar came from the depths of the bag. "That's funny!" said Mr Blair. "The engine sounded peculiar just now. I've never heard it do that before!" He sat listening.

"I hope we're not about to break down," said Mrs Blair. "It would be a long walk!"

But there were no further strange noises and, reassured, Mr Blair let the car roll forward. A few times during the journey he thought he heard that worrying sound again. Was he imagining it? Was it coming from the engine anyway? It was hard to tell with the children continually chattering and banging about. They were far more noisy than usual.

And it was mysteriously hot inside the car. On that cool, windy day with a dull sky, they were forced to keep winding down the windows. Mr and Mrs Blair could not understand it.

16 PROBLEMS

They were home. They were back at school, back in the ordinary, everyday routine. Except that they had a dragon hidden in the backyard. Each day, before breakfast and after school, they slipped behind the wall to visit Firedrake.

The dragon seemed content in his new home, wandering scaly and sinuous through thickets, slumbering under trees, crunching up mouthfuls of blackberry brambles.

Jim and Ellen wanted to show Firedrake to their friends. The children had long arguments about it.

"Rosa and Anna wouldn't tell," said Ellen.

"Peter and Mario wouldn't either," said Jim.

"They'll think we don't want to be friends," protested Ellen. "We never ask them here to play any more."

But Paul and Tania were firm. "The more people who know," said Paul, "the less chance we have of keeping him a secret."

"It's so easy to make a slip," said Tania. "Just a careless word, and people will come and take him away. He's the only dragon in the world! We daren't tell anyone."

"We'll have to meet our friends in the park, or at the swimming pool," said Paul. "It's a nuisance, but that's the way it is!"

At the bottom of the garden was a tumbledown toolshed, with chinks in the wall and no glass in the window. Mr Blair kept his few tools under the house as the shed was too far off and too run-down. But it made a nice little lair for a dragon. When it rained, Firedrake lay inside, dry and comfortable, watching the downpour.

In the middle of the garden was a small pond, neglected and choked with weeds. The children cleared it out one weekend, tearing up masses of dead water plants, dredging out buckets of evil-smelling mud. It was an awful job, but when they had finished, Firedrake had a pool of cool, clear drinking water.

"Whatever have you been doing?" cried Mrs Blair, as they trooped into the house. "Ugh! How did you get into that dreadful state?"

"We thought we'd clean out the pond down the yard," said Paul.

"I'd completely forgotten about that!" said Mr Blair. "Old ponds are nothing but a nuisance. They get smelly and breed mosquitoes. I meant to fill that one in."

"Oh, please don't, Dad!" cried Tania, horrified at the thought of her father striding down the garden with his spade and coming across a dragon.

"We want to buy some goldfish," said Ellen, inspired. "We promise we'll keep the pond clean."

And they did buy several lots of goldfish, carrying them home carefully in plastic bags full of water. But the fish always disappeared after a few days. The children strongly suspected that Firedrake ate them.

In fact, Firedrake ate everything that came his way. Snails and worms, baked beans and chocolate cake were swallowed with equal enthusiasm. Most of the children's pocket-money was now spent on pet food. As the weeks went by he seemed to need more and more.

And he was growing fast; faster than they would have believed possible. By the end of the school term, he measured two metres. Lula remained friendly towards the dragon, but she now treated him with caution.

Mittens, the fat black-and-white cat, viewed the new pet with horror. The first time she saw him she ran up a tree and stayed there all day long. After that, nothing would persuade her to go into the back garden.

The knobs on the dragon's head had sprouted into sharp little horns. The scales on his belly were still smooth to touch, but those on his back had hardened and roughened. It was easy to graze yourself on these, or collect an accidental scratch from his horns or from the barb on his tail. He remained gentle and friendly, but as a pet he had some drawbacks. He was not in the least cuddly.

Jim was playing with Mittens one day, when Mrs Blair exclaimed, "Jim, look at your hands! They're covered in scratches. You mustn't play such rough games with the cat. And I'm surprised at you, Mittens!"

Mittens sat wondering what she had done. Jim hid his hands behind his back. "They're only little scratches," he said.

"You watch out!" said his father. "There's a nasty illness called cat-scratch fever."

Jim went off hurriedly to find Paul. "Is there such a thing as dragon-scratch fever?" he whispered.

One day someone accidentally left the gate in the wall unlatched. Firedrake nosed it open. He wandered past the clothes hoist and in through the open kitchen door.

The Blairs were all out in the front garden. The children were washing the car. Their father was cutting the lawn, their mother was trimming the edges. Lula sat on the drive, watching them. The roar of the lawn-mower drowned any strange noises that might have been coming from the house.

When they had finished, they were all thirsty.

"Come on," said Mrs Blair. "We'll have some lemonade. We've earned it."

They walked round the house and into the kitchen. There was a shocked silence.

Flour and salt canisters were overturned, their contents spilt all over the floor. A chair lay on its side. The toaster had toppled into the sink, the electric jug was smashed.

Mittens crouched terrified on top of the fridge, her fur standing out in a great bristling bush. When Mr Blair tried to lift her down, she spat and lashed at him with her claws.

Under the kitchen table lay a large white bone. "That," said Mrs Blair, "was the leg of lamb for tonight's dinner!"

Mr Blair looked suspiciously at Lula. The dog stood innocently wagging her tail. "It wasn't Lula," said Tania. "She was out there with us all the time."

"She's not much use as a watchdog," said Mr Blair bitterly.

The rest of the house held more surprises. Flower vases were upset, bedclothes dragged half off the beds. Something had sharpened its enormous claws on the end of the sideboard and something had eaten all Mrs Blair's cactus plants. They had been neatly sheared off, level with the soil.

"What could have done all this?" asked Mrs Blair in bewilderment. "Possums? A pack of wild dogs? But surely they wouldn't eat cacti?" The children kept silent. They knew very well who was responsible.

"Come in here," shouted Mr Blair, from his study. "Look at my manuscript!" The desk and the floor were scattered with papers. Mr Blair was clutching a page in either hand. "Look at this . . .

and this! There's another one!"

The pages were brown and crumpled.

"They're scorched!" said Mrs Blair in surprise. "Have you been drying them by the fire, William?"

Paul slipped away. When he found Firedrake basking peacefully near his hut he sighed with relief. The dragon greeted him with a contented rumble. "Don't look so pleased with yourself!" said Paul crossly.

He fastened the gate very firmly behind him and hurried back to the house, worried that his parents might start searching the garden.

"I've checked all over the yard, Dad. There are no dogs or possums out there."

"We must never, never forget to latch that gate again," said Tania that night, when they were alone.

It had not rained for weeks and weeks and the grass was dry and yellow. One Saturday afternoon, when Mr and Mrs Blair were out visiting a neighbour, Jim noticed a thin column of smoke rising from the end of the garden. With a shout he dashed for the gate in the wall, the others close on his heels.

Firedrake was snoozing blissfully by the pool. Just beyond his snout the grass blazed merrily. Paul tore a branch from a nearby shrub and began to beat out the fire. Tania jumped into the pool and swished water towards the flames. Firedrake awoke to see the children stamping out sparks in the blackened grass.

They had two more fires that weekend. The children were frantic with worry. But each time they managed to put out the flames before they did much damage.

"We can't go on like this!" said Tania. "We can't watch the garden all day and all night. There might be a terrible accident."

But suddenly the dragon learnt to control his hot breath. He did not allow it to fan anything dry and flammable. Once, when a tiny fire did start, Ellen saw him stamp on it with his taloned feet.

17 MORE PROBLEMS

"I see," said Mr Blair, on the telephone. "Yes of course, Mr Rossinski. Any time you like." He listened and talked for a few more minutes, then put down the receiver. "Mr Rossinski wants to prune one of our trees. His vegetables need more sunlight. He's coming over here early tomorrow, to tackle two of the biggest branches. He can't reach them easily from his side of the fence."

The children looked up in alarm. What if Mr Rossinski should catch sight of Firedrake?

"He's no right to chop our trees!" protested Tania.

"Nonsense," said her father. "That one's a nuisance to him, spreading right over the fence. He can lop what he likes. It's like a jungle down there."

The children hurried into the garden to talk. "We'll have to move Firedrake," said Paul. "Where can we take him?"

At first they could think of nowhere. The park

was a lonely place, but someone might come along, jogging, walking a dog, or hunting butterflies. The school was deserted for the holidays, but the buildings would be locked and the playground was overlooked by many people's windows. They could not risk taking Firedrake too far. The longer the walk, the greater the chance of discovery.

"I know!" said Ellen suddenly. "The Schneiders are away. They've gone overseas to visit their grandmother. They've got a lovely, big backyard, with trees all round it. It's really private."

But we can't go in there without asking them," objected Tania.

"We can't ask them if they're not here," said Ellen. "I'm sure Mrs Schneider wouldn't mind. I've often been there to play with Maria."

"We're pretty desperate," said Paul. "I can't think of anywhere else. It's only for a few hours and we won't do any damage."

So early next day, in the first, dim, grey light, the children smuggled Firedrake out of the garden and along two streets to the Schneiders' house. They pulled him along on Lula's leash. He didn't seem to object. Perhaps he remembered the walks on the mountain. Now the dog collar would only just fit round his green, scaly neck.

Jim went ahead, as a scout, ready to hurry back and warn the others if he saw a milkman or postman. Ellen followed a little way behind, glancing continually back down the road, watching for strangers. Firedrake trotted along with Paul and Tania, his shining bronze claws rattling on the pavements. He seemed intensely curious, twisting his neck from side to side, gazing at this new world. He poked his head into gateways, but always responded when Tania and Paul tugged at the leash.

"He's getting very strong," said Paul uneasily. "If he decided to go his own way, I don't think we could hold him."

They reached the Schneiders' house without mishap. They went through the little front gate and along the side of the house, then through a tall door, conveniently unlocked. The back garden was just as Ellen had said—a long, wide stretch of grass, completely secluded, surrounded by thick trees and bushes.

"We'd better keep our voices down," whispered Tania. "We don't want the neighbours coming to look!"

They released Firedrake from the lead and sat down on the lawn to watch him. The dragon was excited by the big, open garden. He raced up and down on the grass, stretching his neck, stretching his tail, stretching his wings.

"Those wings have grown!" gasped Ellen in surprise. And so they had. Ribbed and leathery, green on the upper side, yellow beneath, they cast a wide shadow on the grass. The children had almost forgotten the dragon had wings. In the tangled garden he mostly kept them folded at his sides. Sometimes they had seen him in the open spot by the pool, unfurling one wing a little to preen it. But the wings had been very small at first and the children had not taken them seriously. Now they watched and wondered.

They took it in turns to mind Firedrake that day, slipping into the Schneiders' garden when no one seemed to be watching. It meant that Paul was late for breakfast, Tania was late for lunch and Ellen was late for dinner. Mrs Blair grew quite annoyed.

Mr Rossinski had finished his chopping fairly early in the morning. But the children did not dare to bring Firedrake home in the daylight. They had to wait until late at night, when they were sure their parents were asleep.

The others found Paul at the Schneiders', sitting on the back lawn in the moonlight, his hands clasped round his knees. His mother thought he had gone to bed early.

"Come on," said Tania. "There's no one about now."

"Ssh," said Paul. "Sit down for a minute and watch Firedrake. He's been trying to fly again."

And as they watched, the dragon, running and

flapping across the grass, managed to lift himself a few feet into the air and glide along with outstretched wings.

"If he's going to start flying," said Tania in dismay, "we'll never be able to keep him hidden. What are we going to do?"

"We don't know enough about dragons," said Paul. "First the fires, now this! We don't even know how big he'll grow."

"We could find out at the library," suggested Jim. "I read a book about a dragon once."

"That was only a story," said his brother scornfully. "We need proper, scientific books, and there won't be any! Nobody believes that dragons exist."

"We could look at myths and legends," said Tania. "There are plenty of those about dragons. There may be true bits in them, here and there."

The more the children read, the more confused they became. It seemed that a long time ago, a lot of people had believed in the creatures, but descriptions varied.

The dragons in some of the oldest stories had no legs and feet. They were more like giant worms or snakes. Later on, various ones were supposed to have had heads like lions, wolves or elephants, horns like antelope, antlers like deer.

"This is crazy!" said Paul. "People must have

103

been so frightened that they imagined things."

"Well, I don't know," said Tania, "There are lots of different looking lizards, lots of different kinds of monkeys. Why not different sorts of dragons?"

In two of the books they did find pictures that looked very similar to Firedrake.

They could not find out from the folktales how big their dragon was likely to grow. "As big as an ox," said one legend. "The size of a bear," said another. Ellen found one daunting story where the dragon was forty foot long and weighed more than a ton. The children remembered the massive bone in the cave and the huge footprint in the rock by the stream.

"If he grows like that," said Jim, "he won't fit in the backyard!"

The legends themselves were of no comfort either. The dragons in them had enormous appetites; they ate whole cows and sheep and often people. Very few were friendly. Most of them terrified and preyed on their neighbours. They had to be slain by brave men, armed to the teeth and full of cunning.

"Zoom won't be like that!" said Ellen. "He's been properly brought up." She tickled the dragon around his horns. He arched his neck and closed his eyes, beginning his loud, throaty purr. The children were sprawled in the back garden, discussing all they had read about their pet's relations.

"Whatever happens, we're in trouble," said Paul gloomily. "Even if he stays friendly, he's going to grow too big for us to control. If his appetite gets any bigger, we shan't be able to afford to feed him. If he starts flying, he won't stay in the garden. We should have left him up in the mountains, with plenty of space and no one to bother him. He could live in the caves, drink at the streams, munch up his favourite plants and hunt small animals."

"Wouldn't he do a lot of damage?" asked Tania. "We don't want to spoil the bush."

Paul thought for a minute. "I expect it would be all right," he said. "There's only one of him, after all. Dragons must have lived there once, or we wouldn't have found the egg."

"We couldn't have left Zoom up there on his own," said Ellen. "He was only a baby. Maybe he could manage *now*."

But there seemed no way to get Firedrake secretly back to the mountains. He would certainly no longer fit into Paul's sports bag!

The children did not know what to do. They just went on looking after Firedrake, worrying all the time about what might happen. The dragon continued to grow. His green, snaky tail became longer, his legs more muscular. His horns became sharper, his scales had a harder shine. Luckily he never roared. There was nothing to upset him in the quiet, overgrown garden.

Then, just before the end of the second school term, Firedrake disappeared. One morning before breakfast, Jim found the garden empty.

18 AT THE ZOO

The children stared at the Saturday paper in horror. On the front page was a huge picture of Firedrake. He was behind bars in the local zoo, looking very dejected.

In a way, the dragon had trapped himself. He had swooped down out of the sky to catch an ornamental duck on a pond in the middle of the zoo. The people near the pond had nearly died of shock. But a keeper, sweeping the path nearby, had pulled himself together and started banging at Firedrake with his broom. The dragon was so bewildered with this rough treatment that he had let himself be driven into an empty cage. Only when the gate had clanged shut behind him had he suddenly turned and roared at the keeper. It was rather a good roar. The onlookers had been deliciously frightened.

"Of course it's a hoax," said Mr Blair, looking at the paper. "Now, how have they put the creature together? I wonder if there's a man inside that skin?"

"How could it fly if it wasn't real?" asked Ellen crossly. "It says here it dropped down out of the sky."

"You mustn't believe everything you read in the papers," said her father.

"It looks very real," said Mrs Blair, "though I know it can't be! I'd like to get a closer look. How about driving over to the zoo?" The children agreed eagerly, although Mr Blair refused to have anything to do with such nonsense. He went off to work on his novel, which by now was getting rather fat.

Firedrake had been installed in quite a big enclosure, but it was very bare. There were no trees or bushes to hide behind and the ground had only a few patches of grass. At the back of the pen was a long, low hut, where Firedrake was shut away at night.

The dragon had plenty of room to run up and down and to flap his wings, but he could not fly over the steel mesh fence. Round his neck was a heavy chain, the other end of which was fastened to a very stout post. Sometimes he rose a metre or so off the ground, flapping wildly, causing the onlookers to fall back oohing and aahing. But the weight of the chain always pulled him down. He stood and roared with disappointment, making the watchers ooh and aah again.

All this was splendid for the zoo. It had never had such throngs of visitors, or taken so much money at the turnstile. The brave keeper who had captured the terrible dragon was to be presented with a medal. Special excursions were being planned by road, rail and air from all over the country.

"It really does look like a dragon!" said Mrs Blair. "What an extraordinary thing! Where on earth did it come from?" Plenty of people were asking the same question.

Firedrake had stopped flapping and roaring and was sitting looking miserable. From the crowd the children watched him sadly. They did not want to call to him, with so many curious people around.

"We have to get him out of there," whispered Ellen. "It's just like a prison. We must rescue him somehow."

The keeper was enjoying himself. "Keep clear of the fence now," he boomed. "Don't let him puff at you! Now, you've all heard of fire-breathing dragons. Watch this!" He unlocked the gate and stepped into the enclosure. A thrilled gasp went up from the crowd.

The keeper speared a paper tissue on the end of a pole and pushed it under Firedrake's nose. The dragon snorted and the paper burst into flame. The audience went wild.

Jim had wriggled through the crowd and was standing by the gate.

It had two large bolts and a shiny brand new padlock, dangling open from a bracket. In the padlock was a key. The keeper had not yet attached it to the big bunch of keys he carried on his belt.

While all eyes were on Firedrake, Jim quietly took the key and slipped it into his pocket.

"Imagine such a creature loose in the bush!" shouted the keeper. "Think of all those unexplained fires last year! Perhaps we have the culprit here." The crowd began to mutter in an unfriendly way.

"He wasn't even hatched then!" whispered Ellen indignantly.

Jim slipped back through the crowd and showed the key to the others.

"Great!" whispered Paul. "Don't let Mum see it! We'll have to come back after dark, when there's nobody around."

Luck was with the children. When the keeper locked the cage that night he snapped the padlock shut without a second thought. He always kept all his keys on the ring on his belt. He did not realise he had forgotten to add the new one to the bunch.

19 THE ESCAPE

It was a long walk to the zoo. The moon was new and the night very black. The children were glad of the darkness. They tried to keep away from the streetlights, slipping along in the shadows. If anyone saw four children wandering the streets at two o'clock in the morning, they might stop to ask questions.

The entrance to the zoo was on a main road and flooded with light from four high lampposts. The children stared at it from the shelter of some bushes.

"I could easily climb that gate!" said Jim.

"Look at the spikes on top!" said Ellen.

"Besides, there's too much light," said Tania. "Someone might drive past and see us."

"Let's try round the back," said Paul.

They crept along among bushes and trees, at the foot of the high, smooth wall. Around a corner the wall changed to a wire mesh screen. Further on, right away from the road, it became an old paling fence. And some of the palings were loose! Money had been short at the zoo before the arrival of the dragon. All sorts of things, like flowerbeds and back fences, had been neglected.

Tania was able to switch on her torch now, without fear of discovery. The children found two loose palings and wrenched them aside. Paul and Ellen had splinters in their thumbs, but now there was a nice little gap in the fence.

The children wriggled through. They were standing in a sort of shrubbery, and ahead in the dark they could see the faint outlines of cages.

They made their way stealthily through the zoo, searching for Firedrake's pen. It was confusing, starting from the back instead of the front entrance. Not all of the animals were asleep. Behind bars and fences dark shapes prowled up and down; bright eyes watched the children from the shadows. Now and again they heard some sound from the cages, a bark or a low growl. But apart from the animals, the zoo seemed quite deserted. A flock of cockatoos woke and screeched, but no keeper came running to investigate.

They found the dragon's enclosure at last. It looked quite empty. "I hope he's in the hut!" whispered Tania. "What shall we do if they've moved him somewhere else?"

Jim proudly produced the key and turned it in the padlock. Paul slid back the heavy bolts and pushed the gate wide open. The children tiptoed across to the hut. This door was bolted too, but easily opened.

Firedrake lay on a heap of straw, his chain fastened to a ring in the wall. When he saw the children, he jumped up with a joyous roar. The sound echoed round the zoo.

"Look out!" called Tania in alarm. The blast of the dragon's breath had ignited the straw on the floor. Yellow flames shot gaily upwards. The children rushed forward. Paul hurled the water from Firedrake's drinking trough over the blaze. Jim and Ellen stamped on the smoking straw.

Tania struggled to unfasten the chain from the dragon's neck. Luckily she did not need a key. A tricky sort of clip held the links together.

The dragon was beside himself with joy. He nuzzled them eagerly, holding his hot breath politely. He rubbed his rough scales against their jeans. His strange, throaty purr reverberated in the little hut.

"Ssh, Firedrake . . . ssh," whispered Tania. "We have to creep home very quietly." She took Lula's lead from her pocket, half expecting that after the chain, Firedrake would refuse it. But the dragon did not object. He trotted quietly beside the children, across the compound and through the zoo. Paul bolted the door of the hut and locked the gate behind them. They did not want the escape to be noticed too soon.

They had to loosen two more planks to squeeze Firedrake through the hole in the fence. Then they pulled the palings back into place as well as they could.

They hurried home as quickly as possible, trying to keep the dragon deep in the shadows. They were remarkably lucky; they met no one at all on the streets. Once, when a car's lights flickered ahead, they hid swiftly behind a hedge and the driver drove past, apparently noticing nothing.

"When they find he's gone," said Jim, "they'll hunt for him everywhere."

"They won't look in our back garden," said Paul. "They don't know anything about us!"

Tania suddenly had a horrible thought. "Dogs!" she cried. "They might use dogs to track him down! A dog could easily follow his trail from the zoo. Oh, why didn't we think of that?"

They did not know what to do. There were no streams to walk through on the way home and they could think of no other way of throwing a tracker dog off the scent. Morning was coming and they were so tired they could hardly put one foot in front of the other. They took Firedrake back to his garden and crept off to bed, past the door of their heavily slumbering parents.

But the children were worrying needlessly. As

it turned out, there was no search for Firedrake at all. After they had left the zoo, a fire broke out in the dragon's hut. The children had missed one of the smouldering straws and after a while it had burst into flame. The fire had raged through the hut and burnt it to the ground. Only Firedrake's chain remained, black in the smoking ashes. Everyone assumed the dragon had perished in the blaze.

The zoo director was in a fine fury. "Criminal negligence!" he shouted at the keepers. "Fancy bedding a fire-breathing dragon on dry straw! I'm surrounded by idiots!"

20 THE PLAN

Mrs Blair had been collecting old furniture for weeks. She answered advertisements in the newspaper. She prowled through second-hand shops and hovered around auctions. "Next time we go to the mountains," she said, "I'm going to be comfortable!"

A wood-burning kitchen range filled half the hall. The dining room was cluttered with two dismantled beds. A kerosene refrigerator blocked the porch. The Blairs could only just squeeze in and out of the house.

Mr Blair was tired of tripping over things. "It's about time we moved this junk," he said. "We'll hire a van at the weekend and take everything up to the shack."

The children could not believe their luck. Surely in a van big enough to carry all these things, there would also be space for a half-grown dragon.

The Blairs went to a motor hire firm. There were two vans in the yard, a large blue one and a smaller yellow one.

"The yellow one would do," said Mrs Blair. "I'm sure we could pack everything in there."

"You'd be surprised what it holds," said Mr Glogg, who ran the business.

"Oh, no, Mum, no!" cried Tania.

"The kitchen range is too wide," said Paul.

"The fridge is too tall," said Ellen.

"The beds are too long," said Jim.

Mr Blair peered thoughtfully inside the yellow van. "The children just might be right," he said. "We'd better take the blue one."

"You're mad!" said Mrs Blair. "We'll never get that huge thing up over those mountain tracks. What do you think, Mr Glogg?"

"Well," said Mr Glogg, scratching his head. "It depends. You should be right with those tyres and that engine. You could get to most places."

"But the road's so narrow!" said Mrs Blair. "What if we meet something coming the other way?"

"There never *is* anything coming the other way," said Paul.

In the end Mrs Blair stopped arguing. She was very keen to move all her new comforts up to the house in the mountains.

The children were delighted. Back at the house, they raced off into the garden to tell Firedrake he was going home. The dragon seemed infected by their excitement. He pranced around them, eyes shining, his breath a cloud of steam, his lashing tail flattening small bushes.

Then Tania suddenly remembered something. "What about Mad Wally?"

"He'll want to search the van," cried Ellen.

"Too right!'" said Paul. "I'd forgotten about *him*."

"Dad won't want to stop," said Jim. "We could drive past very quickly."

"We'll have to stop to undo the chain," said Ellen.

"Wally might be asleep again," suggested Tania hopefully.

"That noisy van will soon wake him up," said Paul. "You can hear it coming, kilometres away."

The children looked at Firedrake in despair. He flopped down at the edge of the pool and watched them trustingly, his barbed tongue lolling from his mouth.

"We need something to lure Wally away," said Ellen. "Then while he's chasing it, we can drive on!"

"What sort of a something?" asked Paul.

"A cat!" shouted Jim. "He'd be bound to chase a cat!"

"Oh great!" said Paul. "A cat! How are you going to fix that? D'you want to take poor old Mittens up there, and tip her out on the mountain?"

"Wait a minute," said Tania. "It needn't be a live cat. A stuffed one would do."

"Brilliant!" said Paul. "The stuffed cat runs away down the track, with Wally chasing it. No problems!"

"There's nowhere round here we could get a stuffed cat," said Ellen.

"Well, a toy one then," said Tania. "Some of them look very real. We can prop it up in a tree or stand it on the road, then point it out to Wally. It will have to be in the distance, of course."

"How much would a toy cat cost?" asked Ellen. "I don't have any pocket-money left."

"Nor do I," said Jim, turning his empty pockets inside out.

Paul had only a few cents. "But you haven't spent your birthday money yet, have you, Tania?"

"Not much of it," admitted Tania. "I still have ten dollars. I couldn't decide . . . a book, or a torch, or a really good penknife. I was enjoying making up my mind."

"Well, you'd better settle for a toy cat," said Paul.

"It's not really fair!" said Tania crossly. But she did not argue.

Next day Mrs Blair drove the children into town to change their library books. They hung back near the library door as their mother hurried off along the shelves to make her own selection.

"Here," whispered Tania, reluctantly pulling the ten dollar note from her pocket and pressing it into Jim's hand. "There's a toyshop only three doors away. You can be there and back before Mum notices you've gone. We'll pick some books for you."

"You go!" protested Jim. "I'll pick *your* books."

"You wouldn't know how," said Paul. "Hurry up, Jim! Using a cat was your idea."

Jim went very red. "They'll think I'm babyish, buying a toy cat."

"Don't be difficult, Jim!" hissed Tania. "I'm giving up my birthday money. All you have to do is spend it."

"They'll laugh at me," said Jim.

"Tell them it's for your little sister," giggled Ellen.

"If you aren't out of here in just one minute . . ." said Paul, moving threateningly towards his small brother.

Jim went off, flushed and furious. Outside the toyshop he stood shifting from foot to foot, wondering what to say to the shop assistant. Then suddenly in the window, he noticed the very thing. It was a very lifelike cat, covered with long, grey fur. Its motionless yellow eyes stared balefully at him through the window.

Jim took a deep breath and strode into the shop. He put down the ten dollar note on the counter and said rapidly, "It's not for me. Please may I have the toy cat in the front of the window."

The woman behind the counter looked puzzled. She crossed over to the window and peered inside. Then she burst into laughter. "Oh, I'm sorry, dear! That's a real pussy. Come on, Tibs . . . Tibs . . . Tibs!" And to Jim's mortification, the cat that one minute ago had seemed a stiff, lifeless toy, leapt from the window and slunk away behind the counter.

Still laughing, the shop assistant returned to Jim. "Now what can we find for you?" she asked kindly. "We've some very good soft toys. How about an elephant?"

Could Wally be tricked into chasing a toy elephant? Jim doubted it. "It has to be a cat," he muttered.

"Well, there isn't much choice in cats," said the shop assistant. "The one up there's a beauty, but he's twenty-five dollars. The only other cat we have is this one."

"Yes, all right," mumbled Jim, too embarrassed to look closely at the toy.

"That will be nine dollars, ninety-five," said the assistant. Jim grabbed the five cents change, clutched his parcel and ran out of the shop.

The children smuggled the parcel into the car. They opened it later, in the privacy of the garden.

"Blue fur!" said Paul in disbelief. "*Blue* fur!

Jim, you little idiot! D'you think Wally's going to believe that?"

"I didn't notice it was blue," said Jim.

"How could you help noticing?" spluttered Tania.

"There are some cats called Blue Persians," said Ellen.

"They're not as blue as that!" said Paul.

The children stared at the offending toy. It smirked back at them. It had rather crafty green eyes and stiff, orange whiskers.

"There's no time to change it," said Paul.

"It was the only one they had, anyway," said Jim.

Tania kicked at the cat in a fury. She felt like kicking Jim, though she knew she should really have done the buying herself. Her birthday money had been wasted. The plan was ruined. But the others did not give up so easily.

Ellen rescued the toy and smoothed back the blue fur. "It's shaped like a cat," she said.

"It's about the right size too," said Paul. "We'll just have to change the colour of that fur. But we've no more money for dye."

Tania cheered up. "Let's see what we can find around the house."

Half an hour later, they met near Firedrake's hut. Paul had wood stain from the garage; Jim had boot polish from the laundry; Tania had Parisian

Essence from the kitchen. Ellen had been to the bathroom cupboard and found a small, dark bottle, with a smeary label.

"Whatever's that?" asked Tania. "It smells awful!"

"It's the stuff Mum rubbed on Paul's leg when he hurt his knee playing football."

They tried the different things on different bits of the fur. Nothing worked perfectly, but they each argued that their own dye was best. In the end, the children daubed everything onto the toy and hoped for the best. The cat was now sticky, bedraggled and smelly, but no longer blue. Firedrake sniffed it with interest. Tania snatched it away. "He might eat it," she said. "He likes that strange smell."

They hid the toy on top of Paul's wardrobe and hoped its coat would dry before morning. They also hoped their mother would not notice the colour of their hands.

21 HOME TO THE MOUNTAINS

A neighbour helped Mr Blair load the furniture into the van. They packed everything neatly and securely, so that it would not slide around. At the back of the van was a large, empty space.

"You see!" said Mrs Blair. "The small van would have done nicely."

But when the van moved off next morning, following the family car, the space in the back was empty no longer.

Mr Blair drove the van. Mrs Blair drove the station wagon. She preferred to be in front. She did not want to see the big blue van wobbling round the bends on the mountain road. The children gazed out of the back window, watching the van creeping steadily behind them.

When they stopped for lunch, Mr Blair looked slightly worried. "There's something about this road," he said, "that does strange things to engines.

Remember that roaring noise we had last time, with the car? Well, now I'm getting the same effect with this van! It just comes now and again. I don't understand it at all."

"The station wagon's been fine," said Mrs Blair. "I haven't noticed any strange noises."

By midafternoon they were high on the twisty track, between the trees.

"We're nearly there," whispered Tania to Ellen. "Do it now!"

Ellen clutched her mother's shoulder. "Mum, I'm going to be sick!" Mrs Blair signalled to her husband, and stopped the car with a jerk. Ellen had a history of travel sickness. Behind them the van had stopped.

"What's the matter?" called Mr Blair.

Ellen was so excited and nervous, she felt that her threat might easily come true. She leaned against a tree and coughed a little. "I thought you'd grown out of that. The tablets might help," said her mother. "Oh dear! I put them in the green case. Where did you pack that, William?"

While his parents were rummaging in the car, Paul slipped away and ran back down the track, behind the van. He had the toy cat, bedraggled and sticky, in a plastic bag. He stood it upright in the middle of the road, then raced back to the others. "It doesn't look too bad, in the distance," murmured Tania.

In spite of all Ellen's heaving and coughing, nothing had happened. Her mother still insisted on her swallowing a tablet. She grimaced as she gulped down the bitter-tasting little pill, but felt very noble.

As they drove off, Mr Blair glanced in his rear-view mirror and thought he saw a cat behind him on the road. "And so close to Wally's too," he mused. "Perhaps he's right. Perhaps there are a lot of them about."

The car and the van laboured up the steep track and round a bend. There, outside his strange home, was Wally, sitting against the bank, his gun across his knees. When he saw the station wagon, he leapt to his feet.

"Oh bother!" said Mrs Blair. "Now we'll have to waste a lot of time. If only he'd trust us!"

"Halt for security check!" shouted Mad Wally, stepping into the path of the car. Behind him the chain stretched between the tree stumps, blocking the way.

It was very quiet in the mountains. The children hoped fervently that Firedrake would not roar. Tania leaned out of the car window, preparing a little speech, but to her surprise her father spoke first. "Hey, Wally," he called. "I've just spotted a cat, down behind us on the road."

The result was all that the children could have wished. Wally rushed up to the van, his eyes gleaming. "How far down?" he asked hoarsely.

"Not far," said Mr Blair. "Just by the next bend. It was standing right in the middle of the road."

"The cheeky ones are the worst," said Wally, with enthusiasm.

"I saw it too!" shouted Ellen.

"So did I," added Jim.

"It was facing the other way," called Tania. "If you creep up very quietly, perhaps it won't hear you coming."

As Wally tiptoed off down the track, Paul jumped from the car and quietly unlooped the chain from the stumps. Once the old man was out of sight, the Blairs drove on and away up the mountain.

"What a piece of luck that was!" marvelled Mrs Blair. "How lucky that cat was around, just at that particular moment! D'you think he'll manage to catch it?"

The children burst out laughing. "Oh, he'll catch it all right!" said Paul. Then they all fell silent, wondering what Wally would do when he found out he had been tricked.

At last they arrived at the little log shack, high in the mountains. Mr and Mrs Blair sat down in the kitchen to recover, drinking cup after cup of hot, strong tea.

The children quietly unlocked the door of the van and led Firedrake up the mountain. They squeezed past the thorny bush that was trying to grow back over the entrance to the cave. They coaxed the dragon through the passages to the other side of the mountain. Then Tania unfastened the dog collar.

The dragon sniffed the cold, clean air and

looked around him with glittering eyes. He gazed at the distant ranges, the towering rocks and the tree-covered slopes. A rumbling purr began, deep in his throat. Above them on the mysterious mountain the snow still gleamed, as it had done that day when they found the strange, red egg.

"Be happy, Zoom," said Ellen, blinking back tears as she stroked the horny neck. "We'll be back to see you, whenever we can. Don't forget you belong to me. You're my little dragon, whatever the others say."

The others did not bother to contradict her. They stood looking at the dragon, at the haughty arch of his neck, the splendid gloss of his scales, the proud tilt of his head. It was plain that Firedrake-Zoom belonged to no one but himself.

"Good hunting!" said Paul.

"You can grow as big as you like now," said Jim.

"Try not to start any fires," said Tania.

Firedrake stretched his wings, flicked his snaky tail and launched himself into the air. He soared like a bird across the deserted slopes. The children watched him disappear, then slowly and a little sadly, they made their way back to the house.

Mad Wally visited them next morning. He seemed very friendly. "It's nice to know I can trust you people. Between us we'll keep these mountains free of vermin."

"Trust us?" said Tania, confused.

"Well, you helped me get that cat," said Wally.

The children gaped at him. "Did you shoot it?" asked Ellen nervously.

"Felled it with one blast!" said Wally. "My eyes may not be so good these days, but I'm still a crack shot. When I went down to bury the rascal, he was as stiff as a board."

"You're doing a fine job," said Mr Blair.

"I'm winning the battle with the cats," said Wally, "but now the place is getting overrun with rabbits. It's an uphill struggle. No big predators round here, you see. Nothing that eats rabbits."

"You never know your luck," said Paul. "Something just might come along!"